THE DEFTEST DECEIT

SPUD COMPTON #3

I0601127

AMANDA BRIDGEMAN

COPYRIGHT

The Deftest Deceit

EPUB format: 978-0-6482162-9-2

Print format: 978-0-6457363-2-8

Original cover design by
Amanda Pillar of Smoking Hot Covers

Born in Geraldton, Western Australia, Amanda moved to Perth, Western Australia, to study film & television and creative writing at Murdoch University, earning a BA in Communication Studies. Perth has been her home ever since, aside from a nineteen-month stint in London, England, where she dabbled in Film & TV 'Extra' work.

Amanda is a Scribe Award winner, a two-time Tin Duck Award winner, an Aurealis and Ditmar Award finalist, who primarily writes in the science fiction and thriller genres.

Her works include the sci-fi crime thriller, *The Subjugate*, which is being developed for TV by Anonymous Content and Aquarius Films. *The Subjugate* is also being studied at two German universities (Düsseldorf and Cologne) as part of a program on Australian speculative fiction, in conjunction with the Centre for Australian Studies.

Amanda wrote the Scribe Award winning procedural thriller, *Pandemic: Patient Zero*, which was the first novel set in the *Pandemic* board game universe.

She's also written for Marvel in their X-Men universe, as well as for Black Library in their Warhammer 40k universe.

To keep up to date with new releases visit:
amandabridgeman.com.au

Also by Amanda Bridgeman

Aurora Series
#1 Aurora: Darwin
#2 Aurora: Pegasus
#3 Aurora: Meridian
#4 Aurora: Centralis
#5 Aurora: Eden
#6 Aurora: Decima
#7 Aurora: Aurizun
#8 Aurora: Atlas

Salvation Series
#1 The Subjugate
#2 The Sensation

Spud Compton Series
#1 The Darkest Cargo
#2 The Deepest Jungle
#3 The Deftest Deceit

The Time of the Stripes

Pandemic
Patient Zero

Marvel: School of X
Sound of Light

SHORT STORIES

Marvel: School of X anthology
Eye of the Storm

Inferno! Presents: The Emperor's Finest
Reconsecration

CHAPTER ONE

Spelton 'Spud' Compton lowered his head into his hands and exhaled heavily. He couldn't believe this was happening. He'd just looked death in the face not once, but twice, and now he was being asked to do it one more time.

"This is crazy, man," he said, looking up at his brother.

Correction. Half-brother.

"It is, but we have no choice. He'll kill Dad if we don't," Tiberius said, wincing as he rubbed his wounded leg where Spud had shot him. It had been necessary at the time in order to force the hero soldier, the great Tim "Tiberius" Whitlam, to head for safety. And it had worked. Besides, Spud owed his brother a shot in the leg from the time he'd forced Spud out of the military. Call it brotherly love.

"What Guantano asks is impossible," Spud said, referring to the mobster's demands. "Where are we going to get a Panthera-X03 from? We'd have to somehow find the highly secure Quadrant Four, then break into Sector 4, then steal an incredibly dangerous Panthera-X03, then do a deal with the goddamn mob, all the while avoiding navy detection. That is, if we can ever get out of here first," Spud said glancing about the walls of the admiral's ship, the *Gabriel*, their current informal prison.

"If we don't do something, Dad will die!"

"You mean *your* dad," Spud muttered.

"No, *our* dad, Spel. He raised you. He raised you like his own while your *real* dad took off and deserted you."

"Because *your* dad sent *my* dad away from *our* mother!"

"And it was just as well, given how he turned out. You'd prefer to have been raised by a mobster rather than a soldier turned Senator?"

Spud shook his head in disbelief and sighed. "I can't believe my real father is the head of the Guantano clan." The revelation that the Senator was not his real father had come to him deep in the heart of the jungle on Bracken-Loti. The *Benobi* crew had been forcibly teamed with Tiberius' unit, and the two estranged brothers, despite being hunted by several Pantheras at the time, had managed to clear the air between them. Part of clearing that air was Tim telling Spud that their father was not Spud's biological father.

"We have to save Dad," Tiberius said firmly.

Spud studied his brother, ever the image of their father. Tall, thick brown hair, blue eyes, sharp features. Spud looked nothing like them with his blond hair, brown eyes and soft rounded features. He was shorter than his brother too, standing 5'11 to his 6'1, and where Tiberius had defined musculature, ever the soldier, Spud was simply stocky.

"We can't do this alone, Tim," Spud said. "We'd need the navy's help, but if Guantano smells navy involvement, he'll kill Dad." Spud sat back in his chair, mind turning over. "But there's no way we can break into Quadrant Four and steal an X. We need the navy to give us one, and I highly doubt they'll just hand one over to us given we've killed all their others."

"They will for the Senator," Tiberius said confidently. "And if I ask them to."

Spud studied him. "I know you're their golden boy, hero soldier, Tim, but in case it escaped your attention down on Bracken-Loti, they valued the Pantheras above our lives, including yours."

"Maybe the folks on Quadrant Four did," Tiberius gave a nod, "but Admiral Eames has my back. I know it. I'll speak to him. I'm not asking the navy to hand over an X, they're just loaning it to us for the trade. Once we have Dad back, the navy can swoop in, bust Guantano's mob and take back their X. It'll never leave its box."

Spud chuckled. "Famous last words, Tim."

"We're doing this, Spel," Tiberius said firmly. "It's time you stopped shirking responsibility and step up."

"Guantano's not that stupid, Tim. He hasn't built his empire on trusting people, he's built it on killing people. If you're involved, he'll be expecting the navy to be somewhere close by. He'll see us coming a mile away."

Tiberius grabbed Spud's shirt and yanked him right up to his face. "I went into the Bracken-Loti jungle for you, and I will do this now for Dad. And *you* are going to help me. We're all in this mess because of *you!*"

"I was duped by my ex! I had no idea what that cargo was."

"It doesn't matter." Tiberius released his shirt and pushed him back. "It was probably only a matter of time before Guantano tried to reel you into his clan anyway."

Spud scoffed a laugh. "You really think so little of me, that you think I'd go there? Join the mob?"

Tiberius stared at him. "I'd like to think not, Spel, but you couldn't wait to leave the navy, then you got busted for stealing from the navy. The downward trajectory has started."

"I told you, that was my ex. I didn't know it was stolen goods and sure as shit didn't realize those stolen goods contained a Panthera or were headed to Guantano."

"Well, now's your chance to prove it," Tiberius said. "I got your ass out of that jungle, now you help me get Dad's ass out of this. Redemption, Spel. It's called redemption."

Spud stared at him, mind ticking over, trying to think of a way out of this that didn't involve him getting close to another X. His back was already filled with scars.

"If you won't do it for Dad, then do it for me," Tim said, his voice gentler. He was asking as a brother, not a soldier. They hadn't always seen eye-to-eye or even been close for that matter, but something happened in that jungle. A brotherly bond had finally formed between the two. Call it the passing of time, call it the difference between being two different kids who grew into distant teenagers, who grew further apart as young adults, but now in their late 30s had maybe finally grown up and realized what family meant to them.

Spud studied him a moment, then stood and squared up to him. "Alright. I'll do this. But let's get one thing straight."

"What's that?"

"I got *your* ass out of that jungle, Tim. I shot you in the leg so you could get to safety, while I faced that last goddamn Panthera alone. So cut the hero crap, alright?"

That's the beauty of family, right? You can call each other out on their bullshit.

Tiberius stared at him, eyes twinkling. Then he broke a small smile. "I think we call it a draw. I seem to remember killing the Panthera that knocked you down and was about to eat you after it killed Heiko."

"And I came to your defense when that other Panthera knocked you down after Grant was killed. Oh, wait! That means I saved your life twice." Spud grinned at his brother. "Not bad for a dropout like me, huh?"

Tiberius sighed. "I don't want to fight with you, Spel. Not after what we've been through. Let's drop the competition bullshit and just be brothers, huh?"

Spud's grin fell away. He stared at his brother a moment, then nodded. "Okay."

Tiberius held out his hand. Spud eyed it, then shook it.

Tiberius squeezed his hand incredibly tight, almost crushing it. Spud winced.

"I'll always be stronger," Tiberius said, grinning. "Remember that."

Spud nodded, then kneed him in the balls.

"And I'll always be smarter!"

Tiberius bent over groaning. "You little shit!"

Spud swiftly headed for the door. "If you want to save Dad, you better start buttering up the admiral, golden boy, and get us that Panthera!"

And with that, he left the room, smiling.

● ● ●

Spud knocked softly on Lieutenant Eve Grey's door, in the med bay. She sat on the side of her bed, looking strangely mysterious, her blond curls down and floating about her face beside her light green eyes.

"Close the door," she said, "quickly."

Spud did as requested and smiled, wondering what her intentions were. His smile faded when she pointed to the corner of the room, where a mound of shed skin and fur lay.

"Oh shit..." Spud said. "That came from Lulu? How big is she?"

Upon hearing his voice, Lulu's *meow* sounded and she appeared from under the covers of Grey's bed. Her blue eyes stared at Spud while she twitched her ears about, the tufts of hair atop each tip like black antennas. Lulu crawled out from under the covers, stretching, then jumped down to the floor and trotted over to Spud. Where she was once the size of a cat, she now had the build of a medium-size dog. A fluffy, tabby one at that, with big fluffy mittens for feet.

"H-hey," he greeted her, trying to hide his shock at her growth spurt, as she reared up, placing her front paws on his thighs. He reached down and petted her, glancing wide-eyed at Grey.

"McLaren did say she would grow fast, I guess," he said, referencing the scientist they'd met on Bracken-Loti. The one who had created Lulu by crossing a Bracken-Loti lynx with a Panthera-X03.

"It was disgusting," Grey said with a look of repulsion. "I thought some alien creature was going to come out of her. Did McLaren say how fast and how big?"

"How fast I don't know, he just said fast. In terms of size, he said she shouldn't grow as large as a Panthera."

"Spud," Grey said, "you can't hide this. The navy will figure it out and they'll take her from you."

Spud crouched down to the floor as Lulu smooched him, rubbing her body along his with affection, her tail whipping him in the face.

"They won't know unless her camouflage kicks in. I told them she was a Bracken-Loti lynx and they bought it. Which isn't a lie, she's half a lynx. Look at her pointy-ear fur. I'll just say this breed grows faster than cats on earth."

"But the other half of her is an X," Grey said. "You won't be able to hide that part of her, Spud."

He sighed and nodded. "If they see her take on a camouflage appearance we're in trouble."

"And if they find out she's part X, they'll want to experiment on her."

Spud locked eyes with Grey, then stood again. "That's why I'm taking her with me."

"Taking her? Where?"

"I... got something to do with Tiberius."

"What?"

Spud averted his eyes. "Can't say."

"Spud..." She stared at him. "What are you up to?"

He looked back at her. "Don't worry about that. How're you doing anyway? What are you even doing up?"

She stared at him. "You can't keep a good soldier down."

"Yeah, but your back was cut up pretty good from that Panthera."

"As was yours and you hit Bracken-Loti pretty soon after your injuries."

He shrugged. "I healed pretty quick. Guess it helps to have the admiral's best physicians on hand."

"And the healing properties of the X's anti-venom. You know, I think that's why they were always hard to kill. That's why we had to shoot the hell out of them before they would go down."

"Could be," he nodded, as Lulu meowed loudly, then suddenly sprang up into his arms. "Whoa!" he said catching her.

Grey smiled. "She's going to be a handful."

Spud threw Grey a cheeky smile. "As are all the women in my life."

Grey stared back at him, a small smile upon her lips. His eyes lingered there a moment, before he looked back to Lulu and pressed his face into hers as she smooched him again.

"Lulu saved our lives," he said. "The Pantheras couldn't sneak up on us with her around. She's our warning signal." His mind began to tick over as he stared at Lulu, felt her purring reverberating through his chest. "And that is why she is coming with me."

"Spud," Grey's smile fell away. "What the hell are you up to?"

"You just get better," he said. "I'll be back before you know it... and we'll have that dinner you promised me."

They stared at each other for a moment, before he turned to leave.

"Spud," she said, stopping him.

He turned back to her.

"Don't think I'm cleaning up that crap," she said, pointing to the shed skin and fur.

Spud broke out another smile and put Lulu back on the ground. "Yes, ma'am."

And then he moved to clean it up.

CHAPTER TWO

Spud sat in his allocated, though temporary, quarters on the crew deck of the Gabriel, with his remaining Benobi-451 crew members around him.

"So?" Nikita demanded with her hands on her hips, the overhead cabin lights highlighting the lean arm muscles beneath her dark skin. "Are they letting us go or is there a further complication in our release given we killed all their precious Pantheras on Bracken-Loti?"

"Er, well, there's a complication, but I'm hoping my brother is smoothing that out with the admiral now."

"What complication?" Glossy asked as she bit her fingernails, her brown Latina eyes piercing his from beneath her bright-pink, closely-shaved hair.

"Let me guess," Finn sighed, "we now have to kill ten of them."

"No," Spud said, "*you* don't need to do anything, but *I* have to help Tiberius get the Senator back... Guantano's got him."

"What?" Nikita's eyebrows leaped to the top of her forehead.

"Guantano!" Finn said. "He's still in the picture?"

Spud nodded. "He's not happy he paid for a Panthera but never received the goods. He's taken the Senator for ransom until he gets it."

"Gets what?" Nikita asked. "A Panthera?!"

Spud nodded.

"And just where to do you propose to get a Panthera from, Spud?" she asked.

"That's what Tiberius is speaking to the admiral about now. He's hoping we can borrow one to get the Senator back."

"Do you always call your dad 'the Senator'?" Glossy tilted her head as she analyzed him, folding her heavily tattooed arms.

"Only ever since I found out he's not my real father."

"He's not?" Finn asked.

Spud shook his head, hesitated, then unloaded the truth. "Turns out Guantano is."

"What?!" Nikita exclaimed.

"*Guantano's* your father?" Finn asked with disbelief. Spud nodded.

"Did you know this when Shayla asked you to take the cargo?" Glossy asked, brow furrowed.

"No, Glossy. I only just found out when we came back from Bracken-Loti."

"Holy shit," she shook her head. "Does Guantano know you're his son?"

"Oh yeah," Spud said. "It seems everyone knew but me."

"So, wait," Nikita said, "if the navy decides to loan you a Panthera in exchange for your father, er, the Senator, just what do you plan to do once the exchange takes place?"

"I don't know yet. That's hopefully what Tim's working out with the admiral now. But you guys don't need to get involved in that."

His three crew members stared at him. He expected some kind of objection from them, but silence was all he received as the three glanced between each other. He couldn't blame them. After what they'd been through, he couldn't ask them to put themselves in danger a third time. Especially when it involved another X.

"Really," he said. "It's cool. I got this."

"Spud," Nikita eventually said, "you gotta stop changing our job descriptions on us. First we're running cargo, then we're fighting Pantheras, now you want us to deal with the mob."

"I said you don't have to—"

"Of course we will, Spud," Glossy said, sitting down on the bed next to him. She paused a moment, then looked at him warily. "But the navy will be there with their full firepower too, right?"

Spud nodded and threw his arm around her. "Of course. They'll take care of that. It'll be just me and Tiberius who go in. If you guys want to, I mean you don't have to, but if you want to, like, hang back in the *Benobi*, that'd be... reassuring."

"Of course," Finn said, extending his fist. "We've got you."

Spud extended his and knocked Finn's. He eyed the healing cuts on Finn's arms from the Bracken-Loti parrots. "How're the cuts?"

Finn shrugged. "Hey, look, I survived getting clawed by a Panthera, so a few scratches from some man-eating parrots are nothing. Besides, thanks to that anti-venom, they're actually healing fast."

Spud nodded. "Yeah, my back and shoulder is too."

The silence sat for a moment as Spud looked around at his crew. "It means a lot, guys," Spud smiled. "I'll feel better knowing you're there."

"We've got your back, bro," Glossy smiled.

Spud smiled at her and looked to Nikita. She stared hard at him, arms folded. Having Finn and Glossy with him was reassuring, but the truth was, he needed Nikita too. It wouldn't be the same without her. She was his best friend.

"If you ever hook up with another Shayla, I'll break your damn neck!" she threatened.

Spud chuckled. "Never again!"

"Yeah, so," Glossy smiled wider and nudged him with her shoulder, "how's Grey doing?"

Spud's smile grew wider too. "She's on the road to recovery." He stood, moving away from the conversation. As he did, a knock sounded on his cabin door. He answered it and found a young soldier with a serious face, standing there.

"You're wanted in the admiral's office, now, sir," he said.

● ● ●

Spud entered the admiral's office aboard the *Gabriel*. The office was simple and functional but still had homely touches: images of his family, a mounted, signed baseball. Admiral Eames, short and stocky, pepper-haired and mustached, sat at his desk while Tiberius occupied one of the guest chairs. As Spud closed the door behind him and walked toward the desk, the admiral's eyes did not leave him. The look on his face seemed part-concerned, and part-intrigued.

"Tell me your brother is having a joke at my expense," the admiral said.

Spud stood before his desk and shook his head. "I'm sorry, sir, but what he says is true."

The admiral sat back in his chair and studied them both. "You're telling me, you want the navy to hand over an X03 so that you can make a deal with Guantano for your father's return."

"That's correct, sir," Spud said.

The admiral shook his head. "Do you know how much trouble you're in for killing those five Pantheras on Bracken-Loti?" he said looking between them, before looking to Spud. "Not to mention the one on the *Benobi*."

"We understand, sir," Tiberius said, "but you have to understand, the folks at Quadrant Four made a deadly killing machine in the X03. They're not something the navy can easily control."

"They managed just fine until you two came along."

"Sir," Tiberius sat forward, "I lost four of my soldiers on Bracken-Loti. Lieutenant Grey lost five of hers on the *Benobi*."

"And I lost two of my crew," Spud added.

Tiberius gave a nod of apology at the omission. "They come at you fast, sir, and when death stares you in the eye and you have a choice between a tranq gun or a real gun, the choice is easier than you think. Survival comes first."

"That doesn't change the fact that you were asked to bring them back alive," the admiral said. "That was your mission, Major Whitlam, and you failed."

"I know that, sir," Tiberius said. "But the attacks were so fast, they had my men in seconds. We had no option but to stop them immediately to avoid further deaths."

"That may be," the admiral sat forward again, "but we're talking millions of dollars of research flushed down the drain."

"Sir—" Tiberius began.

"Stow it, soldier!" the admiral bit out, pissed. "I know what you're going to say and I'm not disagreeing with you. I hear you about losing your men. *Good* men. It's my job to oversee the navy's soldiers and send them where they have to go, regardless of how dangerous it is. If it has to be done, then it has to be done. I am caught between overseeing and trying to protect my soldiers, and answering to those who hold more power than I. They are chewing my ass for what you did on Bracken-Loti."

"They got their planet back," Spud said. "The X03s are gone and Colonial Ore can move in there and tear the place up," he said, picturing McLaren and feeling his heart sink at his own words. "That was the main mission, to clear the—"

"Don't interrupt me!" Admiral Eames barked.

Spud bit his tongue.

"Sir," Tiberius began again.

"No! Enough! There is no way they're going to let you take an X03 off to space. They won't trust you to get it back alive."

"Out of interest, sir," Spud said. "How many did they create exactly?"

"You think I'm going to be privy to that information?" the admiral said. "I'd heard whispers of Quadrant Four, but I never had it confirmed until Grey boarded your ship chasing that cargo. There are many arms of the navy's defense forces. I deal with the manpower. That's all. I have no oversight of the science or technology arenas. I only know about shit when it is approved and handed to me, ready to use."

"Sir, I know they won't want to give an X to me and Spud," Tiberius said. "If we ask. But if *you* ask... If you vouch for us—"

The admiral stared at him. "You want me to vouch for you? And why do you think they'll listen to me?"

"Because you're Admiral Eames, sir," Tiberius said confidently, "and I'm Tiberius Whitlam. We're two of the most respected soldiers serving, sir."

"Trying to flatter me?" the admiral asked.

"No, sir," Tiberius said, "just stating a fact." His face turned serious. "Guantano will kill my father, Senator Whitlam, if he does not get the X03 he paid for, sir."

"I understand that, soldier. But I can't let you and your brother head out there like cowboys. You need to leave this to the navy to handle."

"If they sniff navy interference, they'll kill him," Spud said. "We need Guantano to think we're being reckless cowboys, sir."

The admiral looked at him. "But you still want our help?"

"Yes, sir, but I think the fewer people inside the navy who know, the better," Spud said. "If we keep this very high level, say, just you, me and Tiberius, Guantano won't expect the navy's involvement. All you need to do is grant us access to Quadrant Four, Sector 4, and give us the cargo we need. We slip in and out, make the deal with Guantano and get the Senator back. We'll return within the week."

"How do you suggest I let you leave here without raising suspicion from my soldiers? You want to stage a public breakout from the *Gabriel*?" the admiral asked amused.

"No, sir," Spud said, "you just give us the keys to the *Benobi* and we'll disappear during the night shift. No questions asked."

The admiral sat forward. "I've been asked to hold you here on the *Gabriel*. You want me to just let you leave here without alerting any of my superiors? Where's my guarantee you'll come back to face the music for what happened on Bracken-Loti?"

"You have my word, sir," Tiberius sat forward too. "Do you trust me?"

The admiral stared at him.

"Do you trust me, sir?" Tiberius asked again. "Do you trust my honor? My loyalty to you."

The admiral considered his question a moment, then gave a nod. "Yes. I do."

"I know you have no reason to trust my brother, but I will personally assure you that we will return the X03 unharmed, and then we will return to the *Gabriel* to face whatever comes next."

Spud looked at his brother, not sure he should be making such a promise.

"I told you, I'd heard whispers only," the admiral said. "I don't have the contacts on Quadrant Four that you think I do."

"Maybe not, sir," Spud stepped forward, "but Finn, on my crew, used to work there. He might. He can give you the names of those who might be able to clear us a path at your classified request."

The admiral stared at him.

"One week, sir," Tiberius said. "One week and *his* ship," he pointed to Spud. "We'll run a smooth and swift operation, get the Senator back and return the X03 before anyone knows."

"You're asking me to put my job on the line," the admiral said.

Tiberius nodded. "I am, sir. But I assure you that the Senator will be *very* grateful for his safe release. You won't need to worry about ramifications, sir."

The admiral sat back again, exhaling heavily. "Shit... This is going to end badly, isn't it?"

"Absolutely not, sir," Tiberius said, standing and throwing Spud a look. "I'll make sure my brother doesn't do anything stupid to jeopardize the operation." Spud stared at Tiberius, making a mental note to kick his brother in the balls again. "And we'll alert you as to when the navy can move in, save the day, and make the arrest," Tiberius finished. "You'll be the hero, sir. Not us."

The admiral sighed heavily. "Alright. So how do we get you on the *Benobi,* without drawing interest?"

Tiberius looked at Spud, his mind turning over, before he looked back at the Admiral, grinning. "I have an idea, sir."

CHAPTER THREE

Spud and the *Benobi* crew walked along the *Gabriel's* hangar, cuffed, while Tiberius and his surviving soldiers, Lorenzo and Byron, escorted them, armed.

"Nice plan, Tim," Spud said. "You're enjoying this, aren't you?"

A big beaming smile spread across his face. "Yes. Yes I am, *criminal.*"

"How's the shoulder?" Finn asked Lorenzo.

"Back in place," he nodded, rolling it around. "Good as new."

"When we get on the ship you're going to tell us what's going on, right?" Byron asked, eyeing Tiberius and Spud cautiously as she held her weapon on Glossy.

Tiberius gave a nod. "This yours?" he asked Spud, motioning the ship.

Spud smiled. "There's my girl, *Benobi-451*."

"She's a bit of a rust bucket," Lorenzo said.

"Take that back!" Glossy said, offended. "She could do with a paint job, sure, but she runs like a dream!"

Lorenzo grunted, unimpressed regardless.

"Yeah, you've done well for yourself, Spel," Tiberius said sarcastically.

"Hey," Spud said, "show her some respect. She's about to help save your father."

"I hoped the navy cleaned up inside after what happened," Glossy said.

"They did," Spud assured her.

"Behind us," Finn warned.

They turned to see two soldiers approaching on a small electric vehicle, carrying their luggage, food supplies and the like. Tiberius moved to the gangway and pushed Spud along to the entry door.

"Code?" Tiberius said, ready to punch in their access.

"Wanna uncuff me?" Spud said.

"Nope. Code?"

Spud sighed. "Mary-Louise 42."

Tiberius looked at him, then burst out laughing. "Your high school girlfriend is your code?"

Spud shrugged. "Hey, she was my first love, turned me into a man."

"Yeah, she was known for doing that to a few guys, Spud."

Spud jerked a look at him. "You didn't?"

Tiberius laughed again as he punched in the code.

"Tell me you did not sleep with my girlfriend, Tim," Spud said.

The door opened, Tiberius grinned wider and pushed him inside.

"I swear to God, Tim," Spud said, turning into the main corridor of the *Benobi*, "if you did... Wait, are you saying she cheated on me?"

"Story of your life, by the sounds of it, Spud," Nikita said, then looked at Tiberius. "Was he always a fool for women?"

Tiberius nodded. "Always wore his heart on his sleeve."

"Oh, I'm sorry if I'm in touch with my feelings," Spud argued, "and not cold-hearted like you two."

"Pfft," Nikita scoffed. "This is why you need a friend like me, Spud. To kick all that trash out the door on your behalf."

"Seriously, though," Spud said to his brother, "did you?"

"Prepare for departure," Tiberius said. "We've got work to do."

"Uncuff me," Spud said, as Lorenzo left to escort the other soldiers to the cargo hatch, further down the dock.

"Why?" Tiberius said. "So you can punch me?"

"Well, that depends," Spud said, "on whether you slept with Mary-Louise."

Tiberius turned him around and pushed him against the wall, grabbing his hands and uncuffing him. "You really think I'd do that? I don't need your hand-me-downs, Spud, I do just fine on my own."

Spud turned around and rubbed his wrists, eyeing him. "Good... Guess that means you'll stop hitting on Grey then."

Tiberius grinned again. "Well, I guess that depends on whether you've been there yet or not. My guess is *not*."

"Tim—"

Nikita barged her way between them. "Both of you, shut the hell up. Go stow the cargo, and let's get the hell out of here."

Spud and Tiberius stared after her as she walked off down the corridor.

"I like her," Tiberius said in contemplation.

"And *she* likes girls." Spud slapped him on the shoulder, chuckled, and walked away. "Bad luck, Tim."

● ● ●

Spud stood with Tiberius on the *Benobi*'s small flight deck watching Nikita prepare for departure as Lorenzo entered.

"We good to go?" Tiberius asked his soldier.

Lorenzo nodded. "Cargo is stowed, but those soldiers were asking questions."

"About?"

"Why the cargo sounded like a kitten?" Lorenzo looked at Spud.

"Spud?" Tiberius asked.

"What?" he shrugged.

"They said they'd heard a kitten," Lorenzo said. "I told them, there must be one loose on the dock."

"You brought the lynx?" Tiberius asked him.

"Her name is *Lulu*, and yes, I did. I don't know if you remember, Tim, but that lynx warned us whenever the X was close. I'm not facing another X without her."

"The X is not getting out of that box, Spel. You won't need her."

"Let's hope not," Spud said, pushing past him toward Nikita. "Get us out of here, Nik. The sooner we're in space, the sooner I can let Lulu out."

"You can't let her out, Spel, she's half X," Tiberius said.

"She'll be fine. Besides, what are you worried about? You've had the anti-venom now."

"I have, but Lorenzo and Byron haven't."

"Nor has Glossy or Nikita," Spud argued. "Don't piss Lulu off and she won't scratch you. It's simple," he said to Lorenzo.

"Jesus," Tiberius shook his head. "So, you losing your mind over women extends past the human race, then?"

"How 'bout y'all get the fuck off my flight deck so I can concentrate," Nikita said.

Spud gave a nod and ushered them out the door.

Spud opened the container that held Lulu. He paused at first, seeing only a bunch of fur, skin and slime, but no cat, but then suddenly she poked her head through the fur and those blue eyes looked at him. She gave a loud *meow* that told him she wasn't impressed he'd put her in a box.

"I'm sorry, honey," he said, grabbing at the fur and pulling it out, studying it with repulsion. "I see you've had another growth spurt..."

Lulu suddenly pounced out of the box and into his arms.

"Whoa!" he said, catching her and stumbling into the cargo dock wall behind him. Lulu was now the size of a large dog and weighed a considerable amount. "Why, honey, you've grown."

She meowed again, still slightly peeved, ears tilting back.

"I'm sorry," he said, giving her an affectionate headbutt. "I had to put you in there to hide you from the dock workers, but you can roam free now." He bent down and placed her on the ground. She meowed testily again.

"I guess you're hungry, huh?" he said, studying her. "A growth spurt like that is bound to do it." He bent down and pet her. "Let's go get you some food."

● ● ●

Spud entered the *Benobi*'s small mess with Lulu trailing behind him. Lorenzo watched her, pausing with a spoon halfway to his mouth, curious. "She's more like a dog than a cat, the way she follows you."

"Man's best friend," Spud smiled as he bent down and petted her again.

"She looks a lot bigger than she was on Bracken-Loti," Byron said, furrowing her brow.

"She grows fast," Spud said, locking eyes with Tiberius. "Anyway," he changed the subject, "looks like we're all here." He glanced at the faces gathered around: Tiberius, Lorenzo and Byron, Nikita, Glossy and Finn. "So run us over the plan, Major Whitlam," he said, turning to his brother.

"Alright," Tiberius said, projecting a map from his data-band. "This is the approximate area of Quadrant Four, based on the information Finn provided." Projected was a rough re-creation of the area, consisting of four individual stations located near each other, but still very distinctly separate. According to Finn, only the very top brass stationed there ever travelled between the four. They were separate entities, separate cities almost, with strict border control, each dealing with a highly classified area of black-ops, science and technology and there was little crossover between them. Sector 4, the area handling biological weaponry, was where they were headed. Finn had worked in one of the other sectors but refused to say which one or what they did there. Finn may be ex-military now, but he still didn't budge on his old classification commitments.

"Now," Tiberius continued, "as we near Quadrant Four, we'll check in with the admiral to confirm he's cleared us a path. That should see us enter Quadrant Four without being blown up. Then we'll see about gaining access to Sector 4 and collecting our cargo."

"They're going to box it for us, right?" Byron asked.

Tiberius nodded. "Yes. They won't want us touching their precious cargo."

"Do you have the details for the exchange yet?" Lorenzo asked. "With Guantano?"

"No," Tiberius said. "First we get the goods, then we'll make contact with Guantano and arrange it. But we'll need to move swiftly. We want to get the Panthera back to Quadrant Four as soon as possible."

They all nodded, minds turning over the operation as they stared at the projection of Quadrant Four.

"I wonder what else they're making there at Q4?" Byron asked.

"You don't want to know," Finn said.

Byron looked at him.

"Put it this way," Finn continued, "they make the kind of things that win wars, but they're also the kind of things that nightmares are made of."

"Just like the Panthera," Spud said.

Finn nodded. "*Exactly* like the Panthera."

"Alright," Tiberius said, bringing their focus back to him. He turned to Nikita. "How long until we reach range of Quadrant Four?"

"If we undertake a star leap, I'd say two days."

"Glossy," Spud turned to her, "how's our star leap system?"

"We'll make to Quadrant Four fine," she said, though she looked hesitant.

"Glossy?" Spud verbally nudged her.

"I need to recalibrate the system as we're lighter without the escape pod," she said.

Lorenzo looked at Spud. "Wait, we don't have an escape pod?"

"No," Spud said. "The navy blew my last one up."

"Is this ship actually certified to fly?" Byron asked, glancing at Tiberius.

"Of course it is," Spud said, glancing at Glossy. "Right?"

She nodded. "We'll get to Q4 fine. If we want to leap back, I might need to take a look at the engine first."

"Why?" Tiberius asked.

"She's just the kind of girl that needs a little TLC to do what you want."

"Spud?" Tiberius looked at him. "Is your star leap system going to kill us?"

"No," he said offended, "it just... sometimes doesn't work."

"Shit," Tiberius slumped. "Will it get us to Quadrant Four or not?"

"Yes," Glossy said adamantly. "I told you that. She may just need some work before we jump back. But, hey, we might not need to jump back. It depends on where Guantano wants to meet us."

Tiberius sighed, closing down the projection. "Just get us to Quadrant Four, we'll deal with getting back later."

● ● ●

The initial star leap ran smoothly, but the subsequent two days were restless. While Lulu shed again—where she was once the size of a Labrador, she was now the size of a Doberman—Spud felt like he was caught in a holding pattern. Waiting to reach Quadrant Four, waiting to see if the admiral had managed to get them access, waiting to see if they had a chance of getting the Senator back. More than that, with the time to think, he now had so many questions about his father, his *real* father, that he needed answered.

Part of him felt it didn't matter. He'd grown up thinking the Senator was his dad, so did things really need to change what he'd always believed? But part of him felt like his whole life had been a lie. He needed to know the truth, he needed to know what happened between Guantano and his mother, and he needed to know why. Why did Guantano leave her and stay away? Was he doing the respectful, honorable thing, leaving his mother to her marriage? Or did the Senator arrange things so the two could never be together? Had the Senator kept two people who loved each other apart? Or had the affair been brief and Guantano just never gave enough of a shit to come back? Did his mother only give birth to Spud to get back at the Senator for his past affair?

Maybe Spud had known deep down all these years that something wasn't right. Maybe that's why his life had been a little more aimless than his brother's. Spud had never felt settled, never felt like he fitted in with the rest of his family—the military men. Was this why? He hated that all this was surfacing now, but there was no way he could run away from it. Tiberius wouldn't let him. Like it or not, he was going to have to face *both* his fathers sooner or later.

"What's going on, Spud?" Nikita's voice sounded beside him.

Spud was standing in the mess, stirring a mug of coffee, miles away in thought. He looked at her.

"Just making coffee."

"Mm-hmm," she said, eyeing him. "I've never seen you so quiet, before. Always yapping and fooling around. Now you're like a ghost. What's going on? Spit it out."

"Nothing, it's fine."

Nikita put her hands on her hips and gave him a firm stare. "You want me to slap it out of you?"

Spud smiled. He could always count on Nik to give him tough love.

"I just got a lot on my mind at the moment."

"Guantano?"

He nodded, turning around and leaning back on the bench as he sipped his coffee.

"It's bound to put your world in a spin," Nikita said, nodding. "But what of the guy? He left you, Spud. However you may feel about the Senator, at least he didn't kick you out."

Spud looked down in his coffee. "You know, I always felt I had to prove myself with him, like nothing was ever good enough." He gave a sad smile. "Guess I know why now. I had to earn my keep. I had to earn my place in that house."

"So, fuck him," Nikita said frankly. "Fuck all of them, Spud. You don't have to prove yourself to anyone. You are *you*, and you got your groove, and if they don't like that, fuck 'em. Listen, my dad walked out on my mamma when I was three. Did I see him again? No. Did I care? No. Dude was a deadbeat. We were better off without him. And you think my mamma didn't have a line of boyfriends after that who judged me? Hell, yes! Did I care? Hell, no! You don't like my ass, you can get the fuck out, man. This is my house and I ain't leaving."

Spud chuckled.

"You are *you*, Spud," Nikita said, stabbing her index finger in his chest. "That's what I always liked about you. You weren't perfect, but you were okay with that. Don't change. Be proud of who you are and don't you *dare* make apologies. You're a grown man now. Be who you are and fuck your daddies' expectations and what they think."

Spud smiled, staring at her fiery eyes. "I love you, Nik."

"Yeah, you're alright," she brushed his compliment away, "but I like you better when you're *Spud*. The wisecracking, gold-hearted, captain of the *Benobi*. My *boss*."

Spud's smile turned into a big grin. "I think that's the first time you've ever called me 'boss'."

"Don't get used to it," she said, then turned for the door. "Now get your shit together and let's get this done."

As Nikita walked out, Tiberius walked in carrying an empty mug.

"What's she fired up about now?" he asked.

Spud smiled. "Oh, nothing. That's just Nik."

"She's a firecracker that one."

"Yes, she is. Hell of a pilot too."

Spud watched as Tiberius poured himself a mug of coffee. It made him think of Miguel, his cook, who'd died during their first encounter with a Panthera. Spud turned to look out the mess door into the corridor, to the place where both Miguel and King had died. His smile faded away.

"I miss Miguel and his food," Spud thought aloud.

Tiberius looked at him. "He's one you lost?"

Spud nodded. "Him, and King, my medic. They died for me." He motioned with his head. "Right outside that door."

Tiberius glanced to the spot and nodded in thought. "Grant died for me." He looked at his brother. "We have that in common, at least, Spel. Our teams will die for us."

"No one else is dying for me."

Tiberius stared at him a moment, then raised his mug to Spud's. "And that we can agree upon."

Spud clinked his mug against Tim's.

"So," Spud said, eyeing his brother, "seriously, did you sleep with Mary-Louise?"

Tiberius broke into laughter. "*No*, Spud. I did not sleep with your girlfriend... But *you* slept with one of mine."

"What?" Spud straightened. "Who?"

"Suzie Monroe."

"Suzie? What? What do you mean?"

"I dated her briefly," Tiberius said, "first year of military school. I came home on break one semester and saw you were dating her. It was too late to warn you."

Spud stared, agape, at him. "She never said anything!"

"And I thought it best not to."

Spud groaned in horror. "Oh shit, I can't believe I had one of yours!"

Tiberius laughed again. "It grossed me out too, brother. Thankfully, you only dated for five seconds, so the awkwardness passed quickly."

"Yeah... She left me for Joe Franko. She thought he was going to be the next big, exciting rock star and I was just going to be a boring soldier."

"I hear she's married with, like, a bunch of kids now. Onto her second or third husband or something."

"Huh."

"And here you are fighting Pantheras and dealing with the mob. The girl wanted excitement, boy did she miss out." Tiberius clinked his mug with Spud's again. "Her loss."

Spud grunted. "Yeah. Her loss."

CHAPTER FOUR

Spud walked swiftly toward the flight deck, having been summoned by Nikita. When he entered, Tiberius was already present.

"The admiral's on a secure channel," Tiberius informed him, then turned back to the flight deck console. "Go ahead, admiral."

"You have clearance," Admiral Eames' voice sounded over the speakers. "I had to pull a ton of strings to make this happen. My ass is way over the line, so you do exactly as I say, understood?"

"Absolutely, sir. What are your instructions?" Tiberius answered.

"When you approach the perimeter of Quadrant Four you will be asked to stop and provide your access credentials. I'm sending these now via an encrypted packet to your portal, Major Whitlam. Only you can access this."

"Yes, sir," Tiberius said, exchanging another look with Spud, before turning back to the console.

"Once the credentials have been accepted, you may proceed to Sector 4," the admiral continued. "When you arrive, you will be searched thoroughly, and only two of you will be allowed to receive the cargo. Major, this will be you and Lieutenant Lorenzo. Understood?"

"Yes, sir," Tiberius answered.

"Once you have the package, how do you plan to contact Guantano?"

"He gave me instructions after he sent the video," Tiberius said. "I'll send a message, then he'll make contact with me."

"How will you send the message?"

"Ah, sir, I think it's best I don't divulge that information for now. I can't risk him detecting navy interference."

The admiral was silent a moment. "You're asking me to hold limitless faith in you, major."

"Sir, I assure you, you can trust me. Right now, I have to do what is right for this mission."

Again, silence.

"Alright," the admiral eventually said, "but you will report immediately once he makes contact. And you will confirm with me once you have the cargo on board."

"Yes, sir. Absolutely, sir."

"Good. Every step of this mission, Major Whitlam, I want you to picture my ass. I like my ass a lot, and I'd like it in one piece when this is over. So every step of the way, you'd better picture my ass, right down to the asshole, and think of ways that you can keep it in perfect health. Do you understand me?"

"Understand, sir," Tiberius said. "I'm picturing your ass as we speak. Thank you, sir."

Spud screwed up his face.

"Good luck," the admiral said, before the comms cut out.

Tiberius exhaled and looked back at Spud.

"Well, holy shit, we're going to Quadrant Four."

Spud and Tiberius remained on the small flight deck, watching as Nikita guided the *Benobi* toward the perimeter of Quadrant Four. Though the ship was very close to the perimeter, all Spud saw through the flight deck observation window was the darkness of space, punctuated by occasional stars.

"Where's the perimeter security?" Spud said. "There's nothing here. Are you sure we're in the right place?"

"I'm at the exact coordinates the admiral gave me," Nikita said.

"But there's nothing here," Spud said, shooting Tiberius a look. "You don't think the admiral gave us a false location, do you?"

Tiberius stepped closer to the window. "If these are the coordinates the admiral gave and Nikita followed them exactly—"

"I did," she snipped, giving Tiberius a "come at me" death stare.

"Then this is where we're supposed to be," Tiberius said.

An alert sounded on the flight desk.

"Wait," Nikita said, studying one of the screens on the console, "I'm detecting a heat signature." She glanced between the window and her console searching for it. "It's... growing in heat... What the hell?! It's supposed to be right outside?"

All three of them stared out the observation window.

"There," Tiberius said, pointing.

Before them a large navy ship slowly appeared, as though an apparition emerging from the atmosphere itself.

"What the hell...?" Nikita repeated, mouth agape.

"Holy shit," Tiberius said. "They can make themselves invisible."

"And not just by sight, but on my scanners too," Nikita said.

"Just like the Pantheras," Spud said quietly, thinking aloud.

Tiberius looked at him.

"Remember?" Spud said. "In the jungle on Bracken-Loti, the Eagle-Eye couldn't detect the Pantheras when they were camouflaged."

"That's why no one knows this place exists," Nikita said. "People probably fly past it all the time—not just the perimeter security, the sector stations too. They're all invisible and they're constantly moving."

They turned back to watch the ship, now fully visible and facing off against the much smaller *Benobi*.

"This is Galactic Navy vessel, *Novatone*," a voice sounded over their comms. "Identify yourself. Over."

"You want to do the honors?" Nikita asked Tiberius. He nodded. Nikita's hands danced around the console, then gave him the thumbs up to speak.

"Galactic Force *Novatone*, this is Major Timothy Whitlam. This vessel, *Benobi*, is—"

"*Benobi-451*," Spud quickly corrected him.

"*Benobi-451*," Tiberius said, "is here on official navy business."

"Roger that, *Benobi-451*," the voice said. "Please send your authority codes. Over."

"Roger that," Tiberius said. "Sending now." He tapped at his data-band, doing as commanded. When he finished, he looked back at the console. "Authority codes sent. Over."

"Roger that, authority codes received. Verifying now. Please wait. Over."

"Roger," Tiberius said. Silence filled the flight deck, before Tiberius looked at Spud, curious. "Why 451?"

Spud looked back at him and shrugged. "Four members in my family, five members on my crew, and my ship."

Tiberius stared at him.

"Authority codes accepted," the voice said, breaking their stare. "Please proceed to Sector 4, the location of which is being sent to you as we speak. Do not deviate. If you veer off course we will be forced to take action. Is this understood. Over?"

"Understood," Tiberius said. "Over."

"Proceed. Over."

Tiberius looked to Nikita. "First gate cleared. Now take us to Sector 4."

"On our way," Nikita said, tapping the screen and bringing up the designated path as she turned the *Benobi* slightly to veer around the large bulk of the battleship *Novatone*.

Just like the navy ship, Sector 4 appeared before their eyes out of nowhere.

"Whoa..." Nikita said. "This is some high-tech shit."

The station before them was a peculiar site. A dark gray behemoth, its center mass was cube-shaped, while surrounding the cube, two large gravitational rings were circling, one this way, one that.

"How the hell do we get in?" Spud asked.

"Guess we gotta dodge the rings," Nikita said.

"Can you handle that?" Tiberius asked.

Nikita threw a glance over her shoulder, insulted. "Please."

Nikita deftly made her way through the swooping rings toward the cubed station. As they neared, they went through the authorization process once more. Once their clearance was granted, Nikita was given strict instructions as to docking procedures and she maneuvered the *Benobi* toward their allocated bay.

"Lorenzo," Tiberius spoke into the internal comms mic, "report to flight deck."

Spud watched carefully as the ship sailed into its allotted bay and the docking crew locked it in place. The dock looked quiet, the *Benobi* was the only ship he could see. Even the docks themselves were empty. He wondered whether that was intentional, to keep the outsiders from seeing anything they shouldn't.

Lorenzo entered the now-crowded flight deck.

"You ready?" Tiberius asked him.

"Good to go, sir."

"Watch your six," Spud told them. "You get in trouble, call me."

"We'll be fine," Tiberius reassured him. "We're just picking up cargo."

"Yeah," Nikita said, "that holds a goddamn Panthera."

"We'll be back in a flash," Tiberius said. "Keep the engines warm."

Tiberius and Lorenzo left the flight deck. Spud sat down beside Nikita and waited until they appeared on the *Benobi*'s external cameras. He watched them approach one of the dock crew, where Tiberius referred him to information projected from his data-band. A brief discussion was held, Tiberius and Lorenzo were thoroughly searched and scanned, then the dockmaster turned and waved something forward. Spud saw two dock workers rolling a large metal box into view.

"There she is," Spud said, as Glossy and Finn entered the flight deck.

"How they doing?" Glossy asked.

"Good," Spud said. "Cargo's right there."

Lulu meowed and squeezed inside the flight deck too.

"Hey, girl," Spud said, scratching her neck.

"You got competition for her affection," Glossy smiled. "She loves Finn."

Spud smiled. "Well, that's good, I want her to be friends with my crew."

"Cargo's coming," Nikita alerted them. Spud turned back to see the metallic box being wheeled by Tiberius and Lorenzo toward the *Benobi*.

"Alright," Spud said, standing. "Let's go get our X."

Lulu meowed loudly.

"Don't worry, Lulu, there's only one X in my heart, and that's you." He scratched her neck again, then moved for the door.

● ● ●

Spud, Finn, Glossy and Byron stood by the open cargo bay door. They watched as Tiberius and Lorenzo pushed the heavy box up the ramp and onto the ship. Finn and Glossy took carriage of it and began to move it to a corner of the cargo hold.

"I'm having an awful sense of déjà vu," Glossy said as she pressed the box against the wall, and Finn secured it in place.

"Yeah," Spud said, eyeing the box. "Me, too."

"So long as the déjà vu ends here," Finn said, finishing up. "Done. Cargo is secure."

"Alright," Tiberius said. "Let's move out."

"Yeah," Spud said, glancing back out onto the Quadrant Four dock. "This place gives me the creeps."

"You don't know the half of it," Finn said.

They exchanged a wary look, then moved to seal the cargo bay door.

CHAPTER FIVE

Spud and Glossy stood silently watching as Tiberius, sitting at the flight deck console beside Nikita, prepped his message to Guantano. They'd decided to have a mixed crew on rotation—one of Tiberius' and one of Spud's—watch the cargo round the clock, so Lorenzo and Finn were taking first watch, while Byron slept in preparation for hers.

Tiberius tapped a key on the console, completing the message, then sighed and looked at Spud.

"Now we wait."

"How long until he replies, do you think?" Glossy asked.

"I don't know," Tiberius said, "but if he wants this X, he'll reply. Still, we can't control that, so let's focus on what we can control. We need to be ready. Us, as a team."

"We do," Spud said, "but we can't really be ready until we know where the exchange will take place. He might request a populated area, in which case the chances of combat are slim."

"Or he requests somewhere out of the way where we're alone. In which case, we need to be ready for combat. Your team is out of practice and your ship is old," Tiberius stood. "Let's start with your ship's weapon capabilities."

"We'll do that, but first we need to do something else that will net us greater results."

"And what's that?" Tiberius asked.

Spud stared at him. "We need to talk to Mom."

"What?" Tiberius' brow furrowed.

"We know nothing about Guantano other than urban legends. We need to talk to someone who actually knows him." Spud shrugged. "We need to talk to Mom."

"Spud, I know you're curious about him and what happened between them, but we can't let emotion get in the way here. This is a military operation—"

"Yeah, well, I'm not military anymore, Tim. This is *my* ship, Guantano is *my* father, and before I face him, I want to know more about who we're dealing with. So, I say we talk to Mom." Spud looked to Nikita. "Set sail for Nirvana Springs."

"Nirvana Springs?" Nikita's brow furrowed this time. "That hippy place?"

Spud nodded. "She goes there this time of year to escape the city on Luna."

Glossy gave a laugh. "I didn't picture Mrs. Whitlam as the hippy type."

"The first thing you need to learn about my family," Spud said, "is that the public face is very different from the private one."

"And she likes to annoy Dad," Tiberius added. "Her stays at Nirvana Springs do that."

"Alright," Nikita shrugged, turning back to her console. "Nirvana Springs it is."

"Er, Spud," Finn's voice sounded over the comms. "You'd better come down to the cargo bay."

Spud tensed and hit the comms button. "What is it?"

"It's Lulu," he said. "Something's happening."

"Shit," Spud said, then raced out the door with Tiberius and Glossy following.

● ● ●

Spud raced into the cargo hold to see Finn and Lorenzo standing in front of the Panthera's box, watching as Lulu convulsed and shuddered before them.

"What the hell?" Spud said, moving toward her.

"I'd stay back, Spud," Finn warned, showing him fresh, bleeding, scratch marks down his arm. "She doesn't want to be touched right now."

Spud looked back in horror to see Lulu's muscles moving beneath her fur, which seemed to be tearing open.

"Okay, she's just shedding," Spud said as she gave a loud growl, much more like an X than the kitten sound he was used to. He'd actually witnessed her shedding before, but she was a lot smaller then. This was a much more dramatic production. Lulu gave a final shudder, then shook violently, ripping the fur further. Spud winced, repulsed, as she finally shed her old fur, stepping away and leaving it behind with mucus and slime, kicking her legs back as she did. The Doberman-sized lynx was now the size of a Great Dane, or maybe even an Irish Wolfhound.

"Hoooly shit," Lorenzo said, staring in awe. Or maybe disgust.

"Talk about growing pains," Finn said, then looked at Spud. "How big is she going to get again?"

Spud looked back at Lulu as she continued to walk around shaking her legs and new fur as though settling her muscles into a new pair of jeans.

"Hopefully no bigger than this," Spud said cautiously. "She's almost the size of a Panthera now."

"But a little leaner," Lorenzo said.

"Yeah," Spud nodded, "that's the lynx in her."

"Those growth spurts aren't normal, Spud," Tiberius said, coming to stand beside him.

Spud stared at his brother. "You think?" he said sarcastically.

"She's becoming more X every day," Tiberius said. "It's dangerous."

"No," Spud said, looking back at Lulu who was now licking her short grey-brown tabby fur. "That's protection."

"For you maybe, what about the rest of us."

"Well, if Uncle Tim is nice to her, I'm sure she'll protect him too."

"Uncle Tim?"

"She's my girl," Spud said motioning to Lulu. "That makes you her uncle."

"Jesus," Tiberius shook his head, "you've got space-brain. Look what she did to Finn."

"To be fair," Finn said looking at his arm, "I really shouldn't have put my hand anywhere near her like that. It's just a scratch."

Tiberius looked to Spud. "If she scratches anyone without the anti-venom—"

"She won't," Spud said.

"I put my hand there because I knew I could," Finn said, mollifying the situation. "I knew I was safe."

They stared at him.

"Well, kind of," Finn said. "Safe from the venom at least."

"You know, I bet she can actually smell the anti-venom in us," Spud said. "I think she knows we're safe. That's why she likes us best. She senses a familiarity with herself."

"It's still dangerous, Spel. She essentially came from Quadrant Four," Tiberius said, "and we don't really know what that means."

"No," Spud said, "one of her parents came from Q4. The rest of her is a Bracken-Loti lynx."

"And we don't really know what that means either. What if the growth thing is the Bracken-Loti lynx part of her?"

"It's not," Finn said. "When the Panthera's box was first opened on the *Benobi*, they found shed skin. The X03 is hairless, but it shed skin just like Lulu's doing now."

Lulu suddenly came trotting over to Spud and they swiftly turned their attention to her. She gave that kitten *meow* and reached up putting her front paws on Spud's chest, causing him to take a step back to steady against the added weight.

Tiberius tensed and placed his hand on his gun.

"Relax…" Spud said to him, then turned back to Lulu. "Hey, girl. Look at you," he scratched her neck and she gave him an affectionate headbutt—her head almost the same size as Spud's now—as she enjoyed her neck scratch, the motor of her purring vibrating through his chest. "You wouldn't hurt your Uncle Tiberius, would you?" Spud took her large face and turned it to Tiberius, "Huh?" Lulu meowed in Tiberius' direction. "Give her a pat," Spud said.

"What?"

"Give her a pat, Uncle Tim."

Tiberius hesitated then reached out to scratch her neck. Lulu tilted her face toward him and closed her eyes.

"See," Spud smiled, "she's just a pussycat underneath all that muscle and claws."

Finn approached and started patting Lulu from the other side.

"And you're sorry for scratching Uncle Finn, aren't you, Lulu," Spud said, eyeing Finn's bloodied arm. Lulu affectionately headbutted Finn's arm, then began to lick the blood away.

"Er," Lorenzo said, "what if she likes the taste of blood?"

"She's cleaning his wound, that's all," Spud said. "She's just apologizing."

"Let's… hope so," Finn smiled nervously.

Lulu had had enough. She leaned off Spud and went down to all fours again. She moved back to her pile of discarded fur and began sniffing it and meowing.

"Well," Tiberius said, slapping Spud on the back. "The first rule of parenthood is that you're responsible for cleaning up their shit. Off you go."

Lulu meowed loudly again. She sounded tetchy.

"I think I'd better feed her first. The growth spurts make her hungry, and lord we do not want a hungry Lulu roaming around."

"No," Finn said, "we do not."

● ● ●

Several hours later, Nirvana Springs appeared in their observation window. Designed to be an Earth-like escape in space, the station was orb-shaped and digitally colored a mottled blue, green and gold for effect. There was no military presence on the station, only minor local law enforcement. It was purely a holiday station for the hippy at heart; the ones wanting to spend their days doing yoga, meditating, eating organic food, and indulging in some pagan rituals he did not wish to think about his mother participating in.

"How long has it been since you've seen Mom?" Tiberius asked.

"In the flesh?" Spud asked. "Months. But we talk over transmission every now and then."

"Mama's boy," Tiberius teased.

"How long has it been since you've seen her?"

"In the flesh? Months."

"And when did you last talk to her?"

"Months."

"But you see Dad all the time," Spud shook his head. "Guess you're a daddy's boy then."

Tiberius grunted.

"Which sector is your mom in?" Nikita asked Spud.

"She's in the Greek sector," Spud said. "She's got a thing for wearing those old robes."

"You mean like a toga?" Nikita said, fighting a smile. "Alright, heading to the Greek sector now."

● ● ●

Spud exited with Tiberius, leaving the others behind on the ship. Nikita and Byron were guarding the cargo, while Lorenzo and Finn slept, and Glossy worked on getting their star leap system ready for another potential jump once they heard from Guantano.

"You been here before?" Tiberius asked, as they moved along a pathway that looked like an Earth street of market stalls. Of course, it was all star-age stuff: crystals, supposedly magical moon rocks, glittery shawls, medicinal herbs and the like. The scent of incense was strong, as was the sweet smell from stalls of organic but laboratory-grown fruit.

"Yeah, several times," Spud said. "It's quite relaxing, actually."

Tiberius eyed him oddly. "Who are you?"

Spud glanced at him. "A man in touch with his emotions, Tim. A spirit freed from the oppression of the military."

Tiberius scoffed and shook his head. "I think you mean soft."

The pathway curved upward as though following the natural slope of a hill. The walls of the station were broken up by large screens that acted as virtual windows, overlooking seascapes and mountains. It all looked very real and very tranquil, and Spud wished he had time to enjoy it. He made a mental note to come back for a holiday soon.

They followed the winding pathway to the "top" of the hill, a place where the most expensive apartments were. His mother owned the third best on the station; the best two belonged to a mega pop star and an ex-president of some poor country back on Earth. Spud wondered if that apartment was where the poor country's money had gone.

They reached the gate to his mother's apartment and pressed the buzzer.

"Yes?" A woman's voice came over the speakers. It wasn't his mother's.

"Is Elizabeth Whitlam at home?" Spud said.

"Who may I ask is speaking?"

"Tell her, her favorite son has come to visit." Spud threw Tiberius an amused look. "Oh, and the other son is here too," he grinned, and Tiberius rolled his eyes.

"Spelton?" his mother's voice sounded. "Oh, honey!" The gate opened, Spud grinned at Tiberius again, then began walking up the white Grecian steps to the front door.

By the time they'd reached the top, the door was open and his mother stood there with her arms out. She hadn't changed one bit. Her short blond hair was stylishly cut, her makeup perfect, and she wore a pastel pink, glittery Grecian-style gown. Behind stood her assistant, a bookish 20-something woman with short brown hair.

"My boys!" she smiled. "This is a surprise!"

Spud hugged her, then watched as she hugged Tiberius.

"Wait," Spud said confused. "This is a surprise? You didn't think we'd check in with you given what's happened?"

"What's happened?" she asked, glancing between the two. Behind her, her assistant's eyes popped and she shook her head in warning at them.

"You didn't tell her?" Spud asked the assistant.

"Tell me what?" his mother asked, looking between the three of them.

"Wait," Tiberius said, "you didn't notice Dad was missing?"

Betty Whitlam stared at him, then turned slowly to look at her assistant questioningly. She looked back at her boys.

"I think we'd better take this inside."

CHAPTER SIX

Spud sat on the couch beside his mother in her living room, while Tiberius sat on the opposite couch with her assistant, their backs to the windows that overlooked the colony of Nirvana Springs below. Inside, the lightning was dim, candles were lit, and a strange-smelling incense filled the room. On the table was a half-drunk bottle of wine and a nearly empty glass beside it.

"So, what's this about your father?" his mother asked, then looked at her assistant. "What haven't you told me?"

"I'm sorry, Elizabeth," the assistant said. "We were hoping to have him back in place before you noticed."

"Before I noticed? Back in place? Where is he?" she asked, then looked at her boys. "That's why you're here?"

"Mom," Spud sat forward, resting his elbows on his knees, "does the name Guantano mean anything to you?"

His mother stilled. She stared at him. "Why?"

Spud stared back at her, trying to read her face. It told him nothing. Maybe that was the botox, though; she hadn't aged for a reason. Still, she'd kept the secret so long, it was foolish to think she'd crack so easily.

"Because he's taken Dad hostage," Tiberius told her when Spud didn't answer.

"Hostage? What? Why?" she asked flicking her face between the two.

"He wants something and he's making Tim and I get it for him," Spud said. "If we don't, he'll kill him."

"Kill him? Get what?"

"That doesn't matter," Spud said. "So, tell me, does the name Guantano mean anything to you?"

She stared at him again for a moment, then turned to her assistant. "Amara, you're free to go for the day."

"Are you sure?" she asked.

"Certain," his mother smiled. It was a smile he'd seen a thousand times before. The practiced one. The public one.

"Well, okay," Amara said, standing. "If you're sure?"

"Have a wonderful night," his mother said, finishing her glass of wine.

Amara collected her things and disappeared through the front door, closing it behind her. Spud noticed his mother staring at the closed door. He knew she was stalling.

"Mom," he said softly, "when were you going to tell me?"

She looked back at him. "Tell you what, honey?"

"That the Senator isn't my father."

Her eyes shone with emotion and she briefly averted her glance. The ruse was up. The truth was out. She took a moment, gathered herself, then she turned to him, smiled sadly and reached out, patting his knee. "Oh, Spel... I never meant you to find out like this."

"I'm thirty-six years old, ma. When were you going to tell me?"

She shrugged awkwardly. "Well, does it even matter?"

Spud looked at her perplexed. "Ah, yeah, it matters. The guy I thought was my father, isn't. You had an affair."

Her face fell a little. "Well, your father had an affair first." She looked awkward again. "It just so happens I got pregnant from mine. Your father could walk away cleanly from his mistake. I couldn't."

Spud felt his heart slice in two. "Mistake?"

"Oh, Spelton, no!" she said, moving closer to him and wrapping her arm around his shoulders. "That's not what I mean. I meant it was an accident."

"Not making me feel any better, ma."

"Honey," she took his face and angled it toward hers, "at the time, I couldn't think of anything more wonderful than having his child. Having *you*."

"But? I sense a 'but'."

"But... then your father found out. Your *other* father. Suddenly he decides after ignoring me with his affair, that he loves me and wants to keep me. He sent your father away. Your *real* father and I never saw him again."

"He never tried to contact you?" Spud asked.

She shook her head and averted her eyes again.

Spud sighed and sat back on the couch. "Did you love him?"

"Which one?" she asked.

"My real father. Guantano."

She considered the question, then nodded. "Yes, I did. He swept me off my feet, Spel. Eric made me feel like the most beautiful woman in the universe." She smiled and nudged his arm with hers, "And, honey, it's no wonder you came along, the way we were at it."

"Gross, ma," Spud said, wondering whether she'd drunk all that wine herself or shared it with Amara.

"So that means you never loved *my* father," Tiberius said.

"Oh, no, honey," she said getting up and moving to his couch. "Of course I did. We just... fell out of love for a while there... but I guess my affair made him think twice about what he had and what he could lose. He made mistakes, but so did I. Your father is a good man and I'm glad things worked out the way they did."

"Are you?" Tiberius asked. "You spoke of love for Guantano, but all you can say about Dad is that he's a good man?"

She sighed. "In the moment, with Eric, I loved him and I believed him. When the moment passed, I realized your father, though imperfect, was the better, smarter choice."

"What do you mean you believed him?" Spud asked, brow furrowed.

She turned her face and gazed out the window over Tiberius' shoulder, lost in memories, a sadness fell across her face like drawn curtains. "I believe he loved me in that moment, but he..."

"What, ma?" Spud said sitting forward again.

She looked back at him. "He quickly forgot me, Spel. Forgot *us*."

"Why do you say that?"

She sighed again. "Spel, why do you want to hear this?"

"Because I need to know! My whole life has been a lie."

"No, it hasn't, Spelton." She moved back to sit beside him again. "Your father, David, had more respect and decency than Eric could ever have. That's why I never told you. Because David would always be a much better father to you than Eric ever would've been."

"How do you know if he was never given the chance?"

She took a deep breath in, relented, and let out whatever she'd been fighting not to say. "Because I eventually realized that I was just a pawn, Spelton. I was just a chance for Eric to get back at your father."

"What?" Spud asked.

"Your father and Eric used to work together closely, but they always locked horns. One day they disagreed so fiercely over something, something that David would never tell me the details of, but it was something that Eric did, that David had Eric demoted and transferred to another position. Eric was upset by this and wanted to get back at your father, so he did it by wooing me."

"He had an affair with you to get back at dad?"

She nodded. "Like I say, I like to believe that he felt *something* for me at the time in order to do so. I mean, *no* man is that good an actor in bed."

"Ma," Spud shook his head.

"Well, anyway, your father, David, found out and had Eric sent as far away as he could. When I found out I was pregnant with you, I secretly tried to track him down. When I eventually did, I sent him a message to let him know, but... I never heard back."

"Do you think Dad intercepted a reply?" Tiberius asked.

She looked at him. "I'll never know." She looked back at Spud. "But over time, word got around that Eric Guantano had left the military and was mixing in criminal circles. I knew then that he was better off out of our lives." Her face softened. "Your father could've ended our marriage and tossed you and me out on the street, Spel, but he didn't. He did the decent and the honorable thing and raised you as his own. He'd made mistakes, realized the error in his ways, and was making up for them."

"Did he have other affairs?" Spud asked her.

She shook her head. "No. Not one," she patted his knee again. "I think my affair gave him a scare." She smiled. "Eric was good for that, at least." She looked back at Spud. "No, he was good for two things, actually."

"What's that?"

"He saved my marriage and he gave me you."

"But you hardly spend any time with Dad?" Tiberius said. "You argue all the time."

Their mother shrugged. "What can I say, opposites attract. We're two independent people with busy lives. Just because we occasionally drive each other mad and like time apart, does not mean that we don't love or respect each other. Let me tell you, there are times your father and I go at it in bed and, oh my *god*, but I won't go into detail because apparently my little boys don't want to hear that."

"No," Tiberius said, "we don't."

"Guess I know now why Dad always gave me a hard time," Spud said. "Because I was never his. That's why Tim was always his favorite."

"Hey, you were Mom's favorite!" Tiberius said.

"Oh, honey," she said, moving back to Tim's side. "I know I over-compensated a little with Spelton, but your father did make him work twice as hard for everything. And he does look a lot like Eric, so your father had a constant reminder that Spel wasn't his. You were always going to be his favorite because you were his. I didn't want Spelton to feel left out. I was trying to take care of both my boys."

The three sat in silence a moment. Spud and Tiberius exchanged an exasperated look at all they'd heard.

"So, anyway, what's this about Eric having your father now?" she asked. "He's not serious, is he?"

"Ma," Tiberius said, "he's threatened to kill him. We believe him."

"But why?" she asked.

"He wants something we have," Spud said. "He's using dad to trade and we need to know what to expect from him. That's why we came here. You know him, ma."

"The Eric I knew was a lifetime ago, far from what he is now, Spelton." She looked at him with sympathy. "I thought he was honorable once, but I was wrong. What he is now? I heard rumors and I didn't want to know anymore. I shut him out of our lives for a reason. I'm sorry but I don't think there's anything I can tell you that will help you get your dad back... but hopefully what I've told you will help you both in here." She tapped her temple. "Maybe it will free both of you of that excess weight you've been carrying all these years and give your spirits room to soar."

"You're not worried about Dad at all?" Tiberius asked with a furrowed brow.

"Of course I am," she said, then fixed her hair. "I'm sorry if I'm a little mellow but I just smoked a Nirvana joint and drank half a bottle of wine. It's hard for me to be uptight when I'm like this."

"Oh god, Mom..." Tiberius lowered his head into his hand.

Spud sniffed the air. So, it wasn't just a strange incense.

"Look," his mother said, "don't think for a moment that your father is weak. Between the military and politics, he knows how to handle himself. And he raised the two of you." She smiled at them. "If anyone's going to get him back, it's my boys."

A call suddenly sounded on Spud's data-band. It was Nikita. He pulled out his phone and answered it.

"What's up, Nik?"

"There's a guy here," Nikita said. "Says he wants to speak with you."

"About what?" Spud asked.

"The X."

Spud paused, then locked eyes with Tiberius.

"We're on our way."

CHAPTER SEVEN

Spud and Tiberius moved swiftly through the Nirvana Springs market, weaving in and out of pedestrians. They expertly ducked merchants carrying large cargo, dodged buyers stopping suddenly to look at wares and leaped over obstructions appearing in their path. Their hurried movement began to catch the attention of laidback passers-by, but no one impeded them further, and the nearer they got to the ship dock, the more Spud's heart kicked up its pace.

"How did they know we were here?" Tiberius asked, reading Spud's mind.

"I don't know," Spud shook his head. "Guantano must've been watching my ship or watching Mom."

They arrived at the dock entrance, bordering the market. Tiberius was slightly in front and he suddenly slowed down and threw his arm in front of Spud to halt him. Spud glanced at his brother curiously, but did as bidden, relegating leadership to the major. Tiberius peered around a corner of the dock wall in the direction of the *Benobi*.

"Two guys," he said. "I can't see if they're armed, they're wearing long coats."

"Interesting," Spud said, "given Nirvana Springs keeps the temperature balmy."

"Isn't it," his brother agreed.

Spud stepped around his brother to take a look and saw the two men standing by the sealed door of the *Benobi*.

"I take it you don't recognize them?" Tiberius asked him.

Spud shook his head. "No. Let's go see what they want, huh?"

Spud went to step past his brother, but Tiberius blocked him again with his hand.

"Approach slowly," Tiberius said, "turn your data-band on so I can hear. I'll stay back and cover you."

Spud nodded, linking his data-band speaker to Tim's. "Just don't shoot me," he said as he walked away.

"My aim is better than yours, brother."

Spud grunted, then moved toward the men.

The visitors saw him on approach and turned to face him. An alert sounded on his data-band. He glanced at it and saw a message from Nikita:

Lorenzo and Byron, just inside the door. Finn and Glossy back a little.

"Good afternoon," Spud called out friendly-like. "I believe you came to see me?"

"Yeah," the taller of the two men nodded. His dark beady eyes pierced over his large, bulbous nose. The shorter guy had a shaved head and a scar through his right brow. They both looked tough, and rough. They lacked military polish. These had to be Guantano's goons for sure.

"So, how can I help you?" Spud asked.

"We've come to collect the package from you," the one with the bulbous nose said.

"And what package would that be?" Spud asked.

"You know what package we're talking about," the scarred one said.

"Do I?"

"Look," the nose said, "we haven't got all day. Bring the cargo out and we'll be on our way."

"Well, see," Spud said scratching his cheek, "we are under *very* strict instructions with our cargo, and I've had no contact to tell me that someone was coming to pick up."

"Well, surprise!" the scarred one said, holding out his hands. "You think we're going to announce our arrival for all to know?"

Spud shrugged. "Maybe not." He pulled out his phone.

"What are you doing?" the nose asked.

"Checking to see if we've had any notifications."

"Uh-uh," the nose said, pulling his coat back to reveal his weapon. "No calls."

"Hey, look," Spud said lowering the phone again. "I've been dealing directly with my cargo's purchaser. I am not handing it over until I have confirmation from that purchaser that you are the ones I'm supposed to be handing it over to. Alright? Besides, no one gets that cargo until we get our payment."

"Yeah, look," the scarred one said, "as soon as we get the cargo safe, you'll get your payment."

"Uh-uh," Spud mimicked the nose. "*First*, we get our payment, *then* the cargo leaves my ship. Now go tell your boss that." Spud moved to the door, then tapped on his data-band: *Let me in.*

As he did, he felt the barrel of a weapon press into his side.

"Give us the cargo or I shoot you right here," the nose said.

Spud turned his face to him. "Shoot me right here, you don't get that cargo."

"You think it's just the two of us here?" the nose warned.

Spud smiled. "You think it's just me here?"

The scarred one glanced around. "He's lying."

"Give us the X now!" the nose hissed, before delivering a hard punch to Spud's gut. Spud groaned and dropped to his knees, winded, as Tiberius fired a warning shot at the feet of his attacker.

"Shit!" the scarred one turned around and fired back in Tiberius' direction.

More gunfire sounded from further down the dock, from the doorway of the next ship. Spud glanced around at Tiberius who was forced to take cover, as other civilians on the dock screamed and ran for cover.

"Dammit," Spud hissed, before noticing the *Benobi*'s doorway beginning to open. Spud quickly rammed into the guy firing upon Tiberius, then spun and swooped through the opening doorway.

Unfortunately, the two men followed, firing at Spud.

Spud raced through the outer bay to the main hold, throwing himself behind a stack of cargo, beside Byron, as she and Lorenzo fired at the attackers.

"More coming from the other ship!" Nikita's voice sounded over the ship's speakers.

"Where's Tibe?" Lorenzo shouted.

"Shit," Spud hissed, catching the gun Finn tossed to him.

The gunfire inside the ship eased. Guantano's two were just inside the cargo hold, taking cover on one side of the boxes, while the *Benobi* crew were on the other. Spud saw Lorenzo motioning to Byron, giving her orders to make a move. Spud shook his head frantically waving his arms.

"Oh shit," Nikita's voice sounded again. "Men from the other ship are going after Tiberius."

Lorenzo looked to Spud. "We've got to help him!"

Lorenzo fired around his cargo at the bulbous-nosed one, while Byron fired upon the other. Byron caught the scarred one in the shoulder. He fell to the ground with a groan and dropped his weapon. The nose, however, managed to hit Lorenzo in the gut. As he did, however, Finn stepped out and fired, grazing the man along the side of the neck. He too fell back, dropping his weapon.

"Jesus!" Spud yelled once the din had ceased, scooting over to Lorenzo, as Byron stepped out covering their two attackers and kicking their weapons away. "Glossy!" Spud yelled.

Glossy ran low toward them.

"Pressure on the wound, now!" Spud barked, then looked to the ceiling. "Nik? Where's Tim?"

She sighed over the comms. "They got him."

"What do you mean, they got him?" Spud asked, panicked. "He's shot?"

"No. They've got him and they're bringing him back to our ship."

Byron looked to Spud. "What do we do?"

Spud glanced around. "We'll trade. Tiberius for these two." His eyes suddenly caught on the box containing the X03. "Finn? Check the box is okay."

Finn nodded and moved to it, running his hands over the surface. "Looks fine."

"Don't shoot!" a voice called from outside the bay doors. "If you shoot, you'll be shooting the Major."

Spud motioned Byron back from the door. She grabbed one of the wounded men and dragged him away, while Finn quickly dragged the other back. Spud put his weapon away and raised his hands as he stepped into the outer bay.

"Alright," he called back. "I'm coming to the door. Don't you shoot either."

Spud stood in the ship's doorway. On the dock, he saw Tiberius standing between four men. Like the other two attackers, they looked mean and unrefined.

"We don't have long," one of the men said, glancing around. He bore short white-blond hair and steely eyes. "Hand over the X and we'll hand over him," he motioned to Tiberius.

"Different plan," Spud said. "Give us him, and we'll give you your wounded men."

The blond shook his head quickly. "No deal. It's the X or he dies."

"The X is destined for exchange with another hostage."

"Which hostage is that?" the blond said, tapping his data-band and projecting an image. "Her?"

Spud saw a picture of his mother looking frightened beside a man aiming a gun at her head.

"Shit," Spud slumped.

"Yeah, shit," the man smiled.

Tiberius' face fell as he stared at the projection of their mother.

"So, give us the X, now!" the blond yelled. "As soon as it's loaded on our ship, we let the Major and your mother go. Understood."

Spud stared at the man. "You hurt her in any way—"

"Now!"

Spud turned to Finn and Byron. "Get the X."

They relented and moved to grab the box, unlocking it from its position and wheeling it toward the exit.

"My brother," Spud said, motioning to Tiberius, as the box was wheeled down onto the dock. Two of the men grabbed it and began wheeling it immediately back to their ship.

"We'll let him go once the box is on our ship," the blond told him.

Spud watched as the scarred one with the shoulder wound got to his feet and followed the others. The leader stood close to Tiberius, gun to his head, as the last of his men moved to help the bulbous-nosed man, whose neck was grazed by Finn. They too moved for the other ship, as the leader and Tiberius began to walk backwards. Spud saw Tiberius' mind turning over, eyeing his captor.

"Tim," Spud called, shaking his head, "don't."

Tiberius looked at him. Spud knew that Tim could easily take the man down, but knew with their mother also hostage, it was a stupid thing to do. "Mom," he reminded him, and saw Tiberius' posture soften again.

Spud looked back inside the ship, saw Lorenzo groaning in a pool of blood as Glossy and Byron did what they could to stem the bleeding, while Nik now stood over them, armed.

"Nik, get a medic," Spud called.

"On it!" she called back.

Spud looked at Lorenzo. "Hold on, man. Help is on the way."

"Where's Tiberius?" he groaned.

Spud eyed the other ship. The box was already on board, then the leader stepped aboard and waved someone in the distance forward. Spud looked further down the dock and saw his mother with two men. Spud's body tightened. Tiberius glared at them as they approached. They passed Spud's mother to Tiberius, then disappeared onto the ship. The leader, keeping his gun on Tiberius and his mother, beamed a smile that Spud could see easily from the *Benobi*. The doors closed and the ship fired up. Tiberius took their mother and moved away to safety before running to the *Benobi*.

Spud watched the ship leave as Tiberius and his mother reached him. Spud hugged his mother while Tiberius ran on board and fell to his knees at Lorenzo's side.

"What the hell is going on?" his mother cried. "That was Eric's gang? Where's your father?"

"Fuck..." Tiberius said, looking at his data-band.

"What?"

Tiberius looked up at him. "I just got a message from Guantano."

"Where the hell is Dad?" Spud asked.

Tiberius stood, his face flushing pale. "He just sent through the details for the exchange."

"He what?" Spud asked confused.

"That wasn't Guantano's men?" Finn asked, stepping forward.

"Apparently not," Tiberius said.

"Then who the hell just took our X?" Glossy asked.

Spud stared at his brother. "Fuck."

CHAPTER EIGHT

Spud gave his mother a kiss on the cheek.

"I'm sorry, ma, but we have to go," he said, stepping back onto the *Benobi*. "Take care of him for us, alright?" He looked at Lorenzo, laying on the dock in his mother's arms. Other onlookers were gathered around now that the confrontation had ended.

"I'll see you soon, lieutenant," Tiberius said to his soldier, locking bloodied fists with him.

Lorenzo gave a nod. "Get that son of a bitch for me."

"Will do," Tiberius said, then closed the door.

Spud felt bad about dumping them and running, but they had no choice. They had to track that ship. Without the X, they couldn't get their father back.

And Guantano would be pissed.

And without that X, their asses would soon be in a navy prison.

And the admiral would be pissed.

"Shit. Shit. Shit," Spud muttered to himself as he marched to the flight deck. "Tell me you got their ship details and you're locked on," he said to Nikita as he entered.

"Sure have," she said. "So, sit your ass down, because I'm taking off."

● ● ●

The *Benobi* took off from Nirvana Springs with speed.

All the while the Nirvana Springs dock officials were blasting "cease and desist" warnings for them to return to the scene of the crime. Nikita soon shut their comms off.

"There they are!" Nikita said, pointing to a blip on the *Benobi*'s radar.

"Give her all the speed we've got, Nik," Spud said. "We need that goddamn X back."

Tiberius entered the flight deck then, his bloodied hands now clean. "Who's on weapons?"

"Me," Spud said, sitting down beside Nikita.

"My aim's better than yours."

Spud glanced at him. "Don't be so sure."

"I bet I've fired a lot more than you have recently."

"Maybe so," Spud said, "but you don't know Nik's flying style. I do."

Nikita cast Spud a questioning look, and Spud held out his fist to her. She smiled and knocked it with her own.

Lulu meowed tetchily from the doorway. Spud glanced over at her.

"I'm sorry, honey, but Daddy's busy right now. You go play with Uncle Tim."

Tiberius looked down at Lulu by his side, who stared up at him with her blue eyes. "He said Uncle *Finn*. Go play with Uncle *Finn*."

"What about Uncle Finn?" Finn said, filling the doorway with Glossy and Byron.

"Glossy," Spud said, "get to the engine room and make sure our weapons are running like a dream."

"On it," she nodded and left.

"Finn," Spud said. "You and Byron assist."

"Will do," Finn nodded and they left again.

Lulu meowed again, annoyed, ears tilting back.

"Tim, seriously, can you feed her before she eats somebody."

Tiberius stared at him.

"We'll call you when the action starts," Spud said, "I promise. Now, please. Your niece." He motioned to Lulu, and Tiberius shook his head.

"Goddamn it, we're about to go into battle. I'm not feeding your cat, Spud."

"She's Loti lynx! Show some respect!" Spud said.

"We're in range," Nikita said, a ball of concentration.

"Alright," Spud said, "let's see if they'll negotiate."

"Spud," Tiberius said, "what are you going to bargain with? They know you won't shoot them out of the skies, because they have the X."

"I don't know yet. Let me think."

"Wait!" Nikita said, eyeing the radar. "What's that? What are they?"

Tiberius stepped closer as Spud eyed the radar. More blips appeared. Blips whose trajectory had them headed directly for the *Benobi*, at speed.

"Who the hell are they?" Spud asked.

"They're not navy," Tiberius said. "If they were they'd have to identify themselves."

"Er, Spud," Nikita said. "They're heating up."

"They're going to fire on us!" Tiberius said, looking through the observation window.

"We can't lose the X!" Spud said, unable to hide his panic.

"We might not have a choice," Tiberius said. "If it was one ship I'd say let's dance, but five of them? No chance."

"You're a poet and you didn't know it," Spud said studying the radar.

"Spud—" Tiberius began to admonish him, but he was cut off as the first ship fired at them.

"Whoa!" Nikita said, jerking the controls and veering them swiftly out of the way. Tiberius grabbed the doorway to stop himself flying across the small flight deck.

"Assholes!" Spud yelled.

"The X ship is running," Nikita said. "Their star leap is coming online!"

Spud stared fixedly at the X ship's vitals on their console.

"No," Tiberius breathed. "No, no no!"

With a flash of light the ship bearing the X vanished from their eyes.

"Shit!" Spud yelled. "*Shit!*" He smashed his hand on the ship's comms. "Glossy, how's our star leap?"

"They're firing again!" Nikita yelled, motioning to the five others. She veered the ship out of the line of fire again.

"We've got to get out of here, Spud!" Nikita yelled. "We can't take on five ships!"

"They're heating up again!" Tiberius said. "Get us clear!"

Then a voice sounded over their comms.

"This is vessel *Saputra* of the Galactic Navy."

It was the voice of an angel.

"Disengage all weapons or we will be forced to fire. I repeat, disengage your weapons or we will be forced to fire."

A smile swept across Spud's face. "Grey…"

"Grey?" Nikita said.

Spud nodded, eyeing the radar to see several new blips headed their way. "God, I love that woman."

Nikita shot him an intrigued glance, then relented with a shrug. "Yeah, she's alright."

They watched as the five other ships began to turn and, one by one, they leaped from space.

"*Benobi-451*," Grey's voice sounded. "I'm on a secure line. Are you all accounted for?"

Spud grabbed the comms. "Yes, ma'am, and aren't you a sight for sore eyes!"

Grey ignored his comment. "Dock officials on Nirvana Springs reported wounded?"

"Yeah, Lorenzo took fire. He's on Nirvana Springs with my mother."

"Alright," she said. "I'll send a ship for him. Stand by, I'm coming aboard."

"Grey," Spud said, "how much do you know?"

"The admiral filled me in on the basics."

"Grey... We lost the X. And not to Guantano. It was someone else."

"You what?"

"The ship that just leaped before you showed up. They had it. That's why we were chasing it. We gotta go after it."

"In that ship?" she said. "I don't think so. We'll handle it. What are you going to do about Guantano?"

"I haven't figured that out yet."

"Has he sent you the rendezvous details?"

"Yeah," Spud said. "Hey, how'd you find us?"

"Admiral Eames put a tracker on your ship. Guess he didn't trust you to handle this alone. I volunteered to follow you."

"You didn't need to do that," Spud said softly.

"Well, it's done," she said firmly. "Now what the hell are you going to do about the Senator?"

"We have the rendezvous details. We'll just have to go there and try and talk him into giving Dad back."

"With what? You don't have an X," she said. "I've got a dossier on Guantano, Spud. He's dangerous."

"I'll think of something," he said weakly. "See if I can reason with my old man."

"Your old man?" Grey questioned.

"It's a long story," Spud said.

"It won't work," Tiberius said.

Lulu gave another angry *meow* then. It was a deep almost-growl, and sounded very much like an X.

They all turned around to look at her. She sat there, whacking her tail on the floor testily, her ears pinned back in annoyance. Now she had their attention she meowed again, low and long.

"Jesus," Tiberius said. "She sounded just like an X then."

"Did you feed her like I asked?" Spud said to Tiberius.

"Wait," Nikita says, "does Guantano know what an X looks like?"

"I don't know," Spud shrugged.

Tiberius smiled at Nikita. "It might just work!"

Spud cottoned on. "Wait, what?!" he said. "You mean trade Lulu for Dad?"

Tiberius nodded.

"I can't trade Lulu for Dad."

"Yes, you can, Spud. And, yes, we will." Tiberius took the comms mic. "Grey, we're going to try and trade Lulu for Dad. Will you chase down that X for us?"

"Spud?" Grey's voice said. "You think it'll work?"

Lulu growled again, hauntingly like an X. She was getting pissed. Spud eyed her.

"Maybe," he said weakly.

"Alright. We'll chase down the ship with the X. You get your father back. And Spud?"

"Yeah?"

"Be careful."

"You too, Grey."

"Don't disappoint me," she said. "Over." Spud stared at the comms mic. He smiled sadly, thinking about Grey's words, how she'd said them before the Bracken-Loti mission and how she'd now said them again. She didn't want him to disappoint her and not make it back alive. God, how he was looking forward to that dinner she'd agreed to. And dessert. *Especially* the dessert.

Spud turned to eye Lulu again. His eyes filled with concern.

"Relax," Tiberius said. "We'll get her back, just like we were going to do with the X. Piece of cake."

"I sure hope so," Spud said, moving toward Lulu.

CHAPTER NINE

Spud stood on the flight deck staring out the observation window at Guantano's rendezvous point—a ship named *Bandora's Star*. She was much bigger than the *Benobi*, a metallic dark gray in color, shaped somewhat like ocean cruise liner, and in the manner of the navy ships near Quadrant Four, she appeared out of nowhere.

"How'd Guantano get the navy tech?" Finn asked.

"My guess?" Tiberius said. "Through money or murder."

Spud exchanged a concerned glance with him, then looked at Lulu, laying on the ground cleaning her fur.

"It's showtime, Lulu."

"You sure you don't want to put her in the box like the X?" Glossy asked, studying her.

"I don't think she's forgiven me for putting her in that cargo container when we first set out," Spud said.

"But a leash, Spud?" Nikita said.

"People walk cats all the time," he shrugged.

"Spud, I don't think he wants a tame X," Nikita said. "He wants a killing machine. Put her in a damn box."

Spud looked around at Lulu. Her blue eyes narrowed as they stared up at him, while her pointy, fluffy ears tilted back a little, like she knew what was being suggested.

"I promise this will be the last time I put you in a box, honey. I swear."

● ● ●

Spud and Tiberius squeezed—with their cargo—onto the small, remote controlled, shuttle that came to collect them. The rest of the crew stayed behind on the *Benobi*, on standby.

Spud and Tim sat in silence for short journey. In part because it was Guantano's ship and he could be listening to them, but also in part because Spud's mind was turning over the fact that he was about to meet his biological father. A murdering, thieving mobster, who had kidnapped the man Spud had been raised to think was his father. Spud had seen Guantano over that video message when he announced that he had the Senator hostage, but Spud was about to meet him in the flesh for the very first time. It was a messed up situation, and thinking about it only messed his head up further. He sighed heavily, exhaling the thoughts, and focused on their destination as it neared.

Their transport docked on *Bandora's Star* and they disembarked inside a small cargo hold. Several security guards dressed in posh dinner suits and armed with tazers awaited them, and subjected them to several pat downs and scans. Spud kept his gloved hands on the box as they did.

Spud and Tiberius hadn't brought many weapons with them, but what they had hidden on their person were swiftly found and removed.

"We'll take the box from here," the lead guard said. He was maybe late-40s, tall, toned and bald, and he looked alert. This was a thinking man's security detail, not just a meathead with a gun.

"Not until we have our father," Tiberius said. Spud raised his gloved hands from the box for the first time, and they saw that he had locked himself to it with a pair of digital cuffs.

The guard smiled with amusement. "We'll have that removed in just a moment." He turned to another guard; younger, dark-haired and skinny. "Laser cutters." The guard disappeared to procure them.

"The deal was we exchange this X for my father. Where is he?" Spud said.

"And which father would that be, Spelton?" a voice sounded over a speaker in the ceiling. Spud looked up at it as he felt the hairs on his neck stand on end. That was the voice of his father. His *real* father. Tiberius glanced at him.

"I've come all this way," Spud said to the speaker. "You're not going to say hello to your long-lost son?"

"Well..." Guantano said, "I guess a drink isn't out of the question. Bring them to my office."

"I'm bringing the box," Spud said.

"No, you're not," Guantano said.

The head guard raised a weapon to him. "The box stays here." He smiled at Spud. "We have a full casino floor upstairs. The safety of our patrons is of the upmost importance."

The younger guard came back with laser cutter and promptly separated Spud from the box. He felt a sense of panic shoot up his spine at leaving Lulu alone down here. Spud pictured Dr McLaren's face, felt another tug of concern. Lulu might just be the last of her kind in existence. He had to keep her safe. That, and he'd grown rather attached to the enormous, fluffy cat.

As though reading his thoughts she gave a low growl.

The head guard and some of the others grinned. "So that's the X, huh? It sounds intriguing."

"Don't stick your hand in," Spud warned. "Keep the box closed or you'll regret it."

"Move," the guard said, motioning them forward with his weapon.

Under the watch of the lead security and three others, they made their way from the bowels of the ship up to the main floor, which, as the guard had said, was a casino with various gaming tables and digital slot machines their flashing lights, small corner bars of different styles playing different music and all manner of wealthy folk dripping in diamonds and expensive liquor.

It looked like a whole lot of fun, actually.

On another night, Spud might've pulled up a chair. It was probably a good thing he hadn't known about its existence before now. Or known that he was the son of the owner. Would nepotism get him free entry and drinks?

They came to a set of stairs covered with plush red carpet like the casino floor and began to ascend. Where the lower floor was bright lights, people and energy, the next floor was all dim lighting and exclusivity. This floor was for the high rollers. The gaming tables, carpets and balustrades were made from premium materials, the entertainment more subtle, the drinks more expensive and elaborate, and it was choking with cigar smoke.

But still they continued to ascend more carpeted stairs.

As they hit the next floor, Spud saw glass cages lining the corridor walls. As he passed each one, he peered through the glass and saw exotic snakes and critters of all kinds—the kind you wouldn't want to cross paths with. It was a rich man's menagerie of rarity and danger.

The lead guard noticed Spud's interest.

"Guantano's private collection," he told him. "Every animal here can kill you. We call it the lethal level," he smiled.

"Okaaay," Spud said, exchanging a glance with Tiberius. "The old man is eccentric. Got it."

They walked down the corridor passing each exhibit until they came to an expensive wooden door upon which the guard knocked.

A buzzer sounded and the door before them unlocked. The guard opened the door and ushered Spud through, but Spud suddenly hesitated as he realized what a huge life moment was about to occur. This was it. He was about to meet his real father.

Tiberius saw his hesitation and entered first. The guard pushed Spud to follow.

Spud reluctantly stepped inside Guantano's office. It was lined with expensive timbers, and almost looked like a museum, filled as it was with artwork, and artefacts in glass cabinets, fish tanks and a single birdcage containing the most exotic bird Spud had ever seen; its feathers containing every color of the rainbow.

The desk placed in the middle of the room was empty. In fact, the whole office was empty of people.

Suddenly a door in the left wall opened and a young, beautiful woman walked through, straightening her hair. She smiled at them as she exited the office.

Then another woman emerged from the room.

Then another.

Spud and Tiberius gaped, jaws dropping.

Then the man himself appeared. Guantano.

Spud froze upon seeing him. It was almost like looking into a crystal ball and seeing what he might look like in 30 years' time. Spud had always thought he'd taken after his mother because of the blond hair, but looking at Guantano now, it was clear to see that Spud was indeed his boy. They had the same build, the same round face, and goddamn if they didn't have the same smile.

"And there he is!" Guantano grinned as he approached. "My junior!" He looked to the head guard. "Doesn't he look just like me, Spencer?"

Spencer nodded. "Uncanny, sir."

Guantano stood before Spud and took hold of his upper arms and looked him up and down. "You got your mother's hair, but the rest is me!"

"I'm kinda hoping our personalities are different," Spud said flatly.

Guantano dropped his arms and stepped back, studying him. "Well, now, you only just met me. How about you drop your judgment for a few minutes, son."

"Well, as they say, first impressions count, and given I haven't kidnapped anyone and held them for ransom, I'm going to go out on a limb here and say we're probably very different."

Guantano laughed. "You got the same spunk as me, kid." He turned and moved to sit down at his large desk, motioning for Spud and Tiberius to sit as well. The two brothers glanced at each other, then did so, taking the guest chairs. "So, this is the great Tiberius Whitlam, huh?" Guantano said, eyeing Spud's brother over. "Last time I saw you, you came up to my knee." Guantano's smile fell away. "You never did like me, did you?"

"I guess some people are like dogs," Tiberius said. "They know when someone is a threat to their family."

Guantano grunted, then gave a sly smile. "Your mother didn't seem to mind."

"She was blinded by your lies," Spud cut in. Guantano shifted his eyes back to him.

"Well, I can see everyone else has told their side of the story. You don't care to hear mine?"

"Where is our father?" Tiberius cut in. "We brought the X, now bring us our father."

"*Your* father," Guantano corrected him.

"*Our* father," Spud said firmly. Tiberius shot him a glance, trying to hide his surprise.

"No, kid," Guantano said, sitting forward. "*I'm* your father." He sat back again. "Whether you like it or not."

"If you're so eager to claim paternity, then where were you all these years?" Spud asked. "You dumped my *pregnant* mother and you ran."

"His father sent me away," Guantano said, hiking his thumb at Tiberius.

"So? If you loved my mother, if you are so keen to claim me as yours, why didn't you tell his father to get lost?" He hiked his thumb to Tiberius too.

Guantano's expression suddenly switched and fell dark, and he sat forward in his chair again. Spud found it slightly terrifying the way his cold eyes glared into his. He was sure his own face had never held a look so dark.

"Because his father," Guantano hiked his thumb again, "turned everyone against me. I had no friends, no allies. In *those* circles, anyway. So, I left. Onto greener pastures."

"So, you admit you didn't give enough of a shit about Mom or me, to take us with you."

Guantano smiled again, though any sun hid behind the dark clouds in his eyes. "Nothing would've given me more pleasure than to take more things away from Whitlam." He shrugged. "But I'd already had his wife and that was satisfying enough."

In a flash Spud stood and lunged across the table, but equally swiftly Tiberius lunged and stopped him.

"Spud, no!" Tiberius held him firm, though Spud tried hard to move through him and get to Guantano. "We need Dad!"

Guantano laughed. "Ah, Tim, so much like your father. Reserved. In control."

Tiberius turned a look of hate toward him. Guantano pointed at Spud. "You, however, Spelton, are passionate." He leaned forward. "You *are* just like me."

Spud's muscles tensed, but Tiberius pushed him down into his chair and turned to Guantano.

"Where. Is. My. Father?" Tiberius demanded, shoulders broad, stance intimidating.

"Sit down, kid," Guantano said. "In case you haven't noticed, I'm the boss around here." He looked back to Spud. "How do I know that you've brought me what I paid for?"

Spud motioned to Spencer. "He heard the growl. You got what you paid for."

Guantano looked at Spencer, then back at Spud. He stared at him a moment and Spud held the stare firm.

"Well, I can see the Senator has brainwashed you," Guantano said. "He's tried hard to turn you into him instead of me. I guess that was *his* revenge." He smiled again and sat back in his chair. "You see, that's what this was all about, Spelton. *Spelton?* What a stupid name. I bet that was to get at me, too."

"Hey—" Spud began, brows furrowed in offense.

"Is that why you prefer to go by the name of Spud?"

Spud's brows smoothed out. He had a point.

"Tit for tat," Guantano chuckled. "Your father envied what I had, so he tried to take me down a peg or two. Busted me for some minor infractions. Started to tarnish my name in our circles. So, in return, I took *him* down a peg or two by sleeping with his wife. *And* getting her pregnant. That was the cherry on the cake, I have to say. Then he took me down a peg or two by having me sent to a far-off post, pushing me to resign from the navy. So, I did. And every moment since then has been leading up to this, Spud. I couldn't believe my luck when Shayla, *your* ex-girlfriend, took my offer to transport a Panthera-X03 to Sailor's Junction for me. And to use *your* ship to do it. It was fate, boy, don't you see? To bring us back together. And finally, I had a chance to rub you in your father's face one more time." He burst into laughter. "His precious little Spelton busted for thieving from the navy, just like his old man. His *real* old man."

"Where the fuck is my father!" Tiberius snapped.

Guantano's laughter ebbed. He stared at Tiberius a moment, then motioned for Spencer to do something. His head guard moved to another door, disappeared inside, then came back with the Senator. The Senator wasn't his usual self – he was bound and gagged, his short gray hair messed about, his face bruised and swollen, and his gray moustache stained with dried blood. But he would live.

"Dad!" Tiberius stood as Spencer ungagged him.

Spud stared at him, and the Senator stared back, his bruised face softening.

"Would you look at that, Whitlam?" Guantano said. "They *both* came for you."

The Senator nodded. "Something you'll never get to experience."

"Watch it," Guantano said. "Don't start getting lippy now they're here."

"Alright, so you can let us go now," Spud said, standing.

"Why the rush?"

"Because I can't stand the sight of you," Spud blurted.

Guantano's face fell, but his words were interrupted by an incoming call on Spencer's comms.

"This better be urgent," Spencer said, turning away and listening. He turned back to look at Guantano, then at the Whitlam clan. "There's a series of ships on approach. Did you bring backup?"

Spud and Tiberius glanced at each other. Had Grey and the navy tracked them down? They shook their heads, feigning confusion.

A call sounded on Guantano's comms. He answered it on speaker.

"Yes?"

"Ah, Guantano! How nice to hear your voice." Guantano's face fell at the sound of the man's voice.

"Jetsu? Is that you?"

"Jetsu?" Spencer straightened, his grip on his weapon tightened.

"Yes!" Jetsu replied. "How wonderful you recognize me."

"What do you want?" Guantano asked. "And how did you get my number?"

"Like you, I have my ways," Jetsu answered. "Now, Guantano, I want to talk business. I'm about to dock on your ship."

Guantano looked at Spencer. "That's you on approach?"

"Yes, yes. Now show your ship so I can board."

"Or what?"

"Or you'll regret doing business with the *Benobi* crew."

Spud and Tiberius glanced at each other curiously.

"And why's that?" Guantano asked, staring at them.

"Because I have the X03 you want. Not them."

"Son of a bitch!" Spud hissed.

Guantano glared at them. "You don't have the X?"

Spud and Tiberius exchanged a nervous glance.

"Then what have you brought me?" Guantano asked.

"Doesn't matter," Jetsu said. "It matters that I have the X you want. Now let me on your ship, so we can trade."

"Trade for what?" Guantano barked, his anger rising. "I already paid for that damn cat!"

"Not my problem," Jetsu said. "Open up and we'll talk."

Guantano stabbed his finger on his comms panel, glaring at Spud and Tiberius. "You dared try to cheat me?" he asked them, physically shaking with anger.

"What goes around, comes around," Senator Whitlam said.

"*You*, shut your mouth!" Guantano yelled, pointing viciously at him, before stabbing his finger on the comms again. "Jetsu?"

"Yes?"

"Permission to board."

"Excellent."

"But if you try anything, I will gut every last one of you."

"Noted."

The comms ended and Guantano looked to Spencer. "Send him back!" he barked pointing to Senator Whitlam. "Them too," and he motioned to Spud and Tiberius. "Lock them all up!"

"Oh, no!" Tiberius said, throwing a fast elbow into Spencer's gut.

"Shit!" Spud said, throwing himself on the guard next to him. Even his father got in on the action, as a small melee quickly erupted in Guantano's office.

Grunts and groans sounded as the Whitlams fought the guards. They were holding their own all right, but they were outnumbered and soon enough Guantano fired a taser at Tiberius, locking him in pain, and that was all it took to shift the balance to the guards. Within moments the Senator had a gun to his head and Spud was forced to let his guard go.

Spud's guard quickly grabbed him and threw him face first against the wall, pulling his arms behind his back.

"Lock them up and throw the key in with the taipan!" Guantano said. Spud's guard turned him around to face Guantano, who moved right up to Spud's now bleeding face. "I have to say... you're a *real* disappointment, son."

"Disappointment doesn't even cover what you are to me," Spud replied coldly.

Guantano slapped him hard. "Do *not* disrespect me!"

Spud groaned and looked back at Guantano. "I'm pretty sure that's child abuse."

"Lock them up!" Guantano yelled. "Let's go get my X!"

CHAPTER TEN

Spud, Tiberius and Senator Whitlam were on their knees in front of Guantano's desk, their hands restrained behind their backs with plastic ties, while two of Guantano's men watched them with weapons drawn.

"So," Senator Whitlam said to his sons, "there's a Plan B, right?"

Tiberius looked at his father, then turned to Spud. "Er... the navy might..."

"Might?" the Senator asked.

"Grey will find us," Spud said confidently, then shrugged. "Whether we're actually dead by then, I can't say."

"Shit," the Senator said. "So, what did you bring him to trade then if it's not the X?"

Spud eyed the men behind them. "Nothing of consequence."

One of the guards, a curly-haired guy with a thick neck, gave a smirk as his comms rang. He answered it.

"Yeah?" he said eyeing them, then nodded to himself and moved to a screen on Guantano's desk. He swiveled it toward them and turned it on, hitting keys, as various streams of security footage appeared. They saw the different casino floors, the kitchen, the carpeted corridors, then finally found the one showing the cargo hold. "Yeah, I see 'em."

"Shit..." Spud said, feeling his body tighten. There on the screen was Nikita, Finn, Glossy and Byron being marched onto the ship at gunpoint.

"And now he has your friends, too," the Senator sighed.

"I told you before, they're not my friends," Spud said, looking at him. "They're my family."

The Senator studied him in return.

They turned back to the screen and watched across the different cameras as the *Benobi* crew left the cargo hold with some of the guards and made their way along a corridor, coming to a stop outside an elevator shaft, while on another camera, Guantano appeared in the cargo hold and began investigating Lulu's box.

"They can't open it, right?" Tiberius asked him.

"Depends if they can crack the coded lock Glossy put on it."

"I don't know, Spud," Tiberius said. "Guantano seems to have access to some highly specialized tech."

Spud's muscles tensed even further.

"What's in there?" their father asked.

With their eyes fixed on the cargo hold screen, the doors to the external bay opened once more and there was the box containing the Panthera-X03 being rolled in. Guantano stepped toward it, running his hand alongside the box, as another man, who Spud assumed was Jetsu, entered the cargo hold with his entourage. The two men shook hands before words were spoken. Words that soon made Guantano angry. Spud could see he was raising his voice at Jetsu, could see him thump his hand on the X's box and point in the man's face.

"Jesus," Spud said. "They're going to open the box, aren't they?"

"Of course," Tiberius said. "He didn't buy an X to leave it in there."

"I mean, they're going to open it here, now, on the ship."

Tiberius looked to the guards watching over them. "If he opens that box on this ship, everyone will die."

The guards smirked and glanced at each other.

"No seriously," Spud said. "We know. We've fought several Xs before."

"And yet here you stand," the curly-haired guard smiled.

"I don't know if you noticed or not," the other guard, a boxy guy with a crew cut said, "but Mr. Guantano knows how to handle dangerous animals."

"Yeah," Spud said, "I saw the little zoo outside. But a venomous snake has nothing on a goddamn Panthera-X03!"

"You've seen a jaguar, right?" Tiberius asked them. "Well, picture that but bigger, stronger, and camouflaged. That's an X."

"You forgot the jaws and claws, and the lethal venom they release through those claws," Spud added.

"Yeah," Tiberius said. "Venom that we're now both immune to, but you're not."

"So, we'll get immune," the curly-haired guy sniffed.

"Only after you've been in a coma for a couple of days," Spud said.

The two guards exchanged an unsure glance.

"Please," Tiberius pleaded with them. "Tell them not to open the—"

Bright flashes suddenly popped on the screen and they immediately turned their eyes back to it. Chaos filled the cargo hold as Jetsu and Guantano's men fired at each other. Guantano's men appeared to have upgraded their tazers to real guns for Jetsu's visit. Thankfully ship hulls were built to withstand such weapons these days.

"My god..." the Senator said.

Spud saw Guantano escape out the door to the corridor while bodies fell to the ground, mostly his men, as Jetsu laughed and backed up through the doors into his own ship. They watched as Jetsu held up a remote device, aiming it at the X's box, and pressed a button. Another bright flash occurred, and a puff of smoke appeared around the X's box.

"Oh, fuck..." Spud said. "He didn't. Tell me he didn't!"

The doors closed and Jetsu disappeared. They watched in silence as the smoke in the cargo hold cleared. They saw the lock on the box had been blown and the X was stirring, the box moving.

"Oh, fuck," Tiberius said, the color draining from his face. "He did."

"What's happening?" the Senator asked, darting his eyes between the monitor and his sons.

"They just released a Panthera-X03 on the ship," Spud said, eyes fixed on the screen.

"So, what do we do?" the Senator asked.

Spud, heart racing, turned to his father. "We run." He looked back to the guards. "Untie us now!" he said desperately.

"No!" the curly-haired one said raising his weapon. "Guantano said to lock you up, so you're staying locked-up."

Spud looked back to the screen to see a large, furless, clawed paw appear in the hole made from the small controlled explosion. With a few powerful swipes the hole got bigger and the lid suddenly retracted back altogether.

"Oh shiiiiit," Spud said, watching as the Panthera peered over the top of the box. Seeing its pink fetal skin and those dark eyes which sat beneath that skin, sent a tremor of fear down Spud's spine. The Panthera's nose sniffed the air a moment, before ducking down then suddenly springing out of the box. Its feet hit the floor and its camouflage blinked on an off, making it all but disappear briefly.

"Evacuate the ship now!" Tiberius barked at the guard.

The guards looked at each other. "Relax. They'll take care of it," the crew cut said, although his voice was not exactly confident as he stared at the screen in shock.

"Do you carry tranq guns on here?" Tiberius asked.

The guard nodded. "Guantano uses it on the animals from time to time."

Spud watched as the Panthera sniffed the air again and moved over to Lulu's box.

"Oh shit," Spud said again, suddenly standing.

"Get back down!" the curly-haired guard yelled, but Spud ignored him, watching intently as the Panthera moved around Lulu's box sniffing.

It growled.

Then Lulu's box rattled back in response.

The Panthera growled more viciously and swiped at the box.

"Hey!" Spud yelled at the screen. "Get away from her, you *bitch*!"

Suddenly the Panthera's ears flattened and it looked toward the doorway that led to the corridor. Its body tensed and lowered to the ground as it quickly slunk toward the door, engaging its camouflage.

"Who's headed toward the cargo hold?" Spud asked the guard. "You gotta stop them!"

The guards looked dumbfounded at each other, not sure what to do.

On screen, the miraged Panthera suddenly pounced through the doorway and blood splattered back onto the door.

"Shit!" the crew cut said.

"Evacuate the ship, *now*!" Tiberius yelled at them.

Finally, the curly-haired guy got on his comms.

"Yeah, we got a problem. The X is on the loose and it just ate someone."

Suddenly a series of explosions sounded, rattling the ship and sending one or two artworks falling off the walls, before the room plunged into darkness.

"What the hell was that?" Spud asked, as the emergency lighting blinked on.

"Crap!" the curly-haired guy hissed. He switched the channel on the monitor to the main casino floor and saw people screaming and running in every direction. "Do you read? Over?" He ended his comms and turned to the crew cut. "Comms are down! Must've been Jetsu." He waved the crew cut guy to follow him. "Come on!" he said. "We gotta find Guantano."

"Hey!" Spud yelled as they ran to the door. "What about us? Untie us!"

"You stay here!" the guard pointed at him, then they disappeared, locking the door behind them.

"Oh, great!" Spud said sarcastically. "Jetsu's disabled the ship, a Panthera's on the loose, and we're just left here tied up!"

"At least the door is locked," the Senator said.

"The Panthera will find a way around that."

"Spud," Tiberius said, running to the corner of the room, "shut up and help me with this."

Spud turned to see his brother staring into one of the glass cabinets. It was about waist high and held some kind of samurai-type sword. He raced to his brother's side.

"We're going to have to smash it," Tiberius said.

"You think?" Spud said sarcastically. "Just do it! Who gives a shit about Guantano's property. He can claim it on insurance."

Tiberius threw him an unamused look then glanced around. "Break it with what?"

Spud moved to the desk, backed up to a vase and picked it up. He moved back to the glass case and tried to throw it at the glass, but with his hands behind his back, it was a difficult thing to do.

"Throw it from back here, you fool!" the Senator said. "It's all about trajectory. Did I teach you two nothing? Move!"

Spud saw his father was holding a heavy cigar case, and he and Tiberius swiftly stepped aside as the Senator sent the case flying. It landed on the top of the glass and cracked it, but it did not break.

"Shit," Tiberius said, then looked at Spud. "Use your head. Yours is thicker than mine."

Spud looked at him. "Unlikely," he said, but he bent slightly over the cracked cabinet where the cigar case sat and jumped, throwing his body weight on it, shoulder first. The case broke. Spud stepped back, hissing at the fresh cuts across his torso.

"Told you your head was thicker than mine," Tiberius said as he kicked in the now fractured sides and cleared a path for him to turn around and reach in backwards to grab the sword. After a few fumbled attempts and some hissing at his cut fingers, he finally laid his fingers upon the sword.

"Got it!" he said, pulling it out and turning his back to Spud. "Take off its sheath and hold it while I cut my ties."

"Yes, sir," Spud said sardonically.

"Look, I'm the older brother," Tiberius said. "It's my job to boss you around, so do it!"

"Both of you shut up and get on with it!" the Senator berated them.

Spud grabbed the sheath and pulled it off, then took the sword as Tiberius began to run his ties up and down the blade.

"Well, this is awkward..." Spud said, trying to hold the sword against his brother's rhythmic movement.

"Hurry up!" the Senator barked, glancing between them and the screen.

"What's happening?" Spud asked.

The Senator watched open-mouthed. "Jesus! The cat's eating people! How many can it eat?!"

"It's not eating," Spud said. "It's hunting. They're designed to hunt and destroy threats."

"Why are we a threat?"

Spud shrugged. "Why not?"

"Got it!" Tiberius yelled, yanking his body forward and severing the last of his bindings with the blade. "Turn around!" he ordered Spud, dropping his cut plastic tie and grabbing the sword.

Within moments, Tiberius had freed both Spud and their father.

"So, what now?" the Senator asked, rubbing his wrists. "The door's locked."

Tiberius, still carrying the sword, ran to the door the women had come out of and peered in. "Bathroom and bedroom."

"What about the air vents?" the Senator asked.

Spud looked up at the one in the office's ceiling above the desk. "Yeah, the Panthera used that on the *Benobi*. I'm not sure I want to be stuck up there with one."

"Well, it's not up there now, it's on the casino floor," the Senator pointed to the screen.

"We need to get out of here, Spud," Tiberius said, jumping up on the desk, and pulling down the grate covering. "We only need to stay in there long enough to get on the other side of the door. Boost me!"

The Senator climbed up on the desk, taking the sword from Tiberius as he jumped up and grabbed the sides of the vent shaft. The Senator grabbed his legs and helped boost Tiberius up to the crawl space. Spud watched as Tiberius' legs disappeared into the hole, then his arms hung down to take the sword, then pull up the Senator.

"Spud! Help him!" Tiberius hissed.

Spud took one last look at the screen to see the Panthera mow down more well-dressed, unarmed people trying to make a run for it, then he leaped up on the desk, heaved his old man up through the hole, then saw Tiberius' arms reach down for him.

CHAPTER ELEVEN

Spud watched as Tiberius peered down through the air vent on the outside of the office. Spud could hear running footsteps, could hear yelling and screaming in the distance. Then the sounds faded away.

"We need to find Nik and the others," Spud whispered, tapping at his data-band. "Comms are still down. Jetsu got Guantano real good, huh?"

"Yeah," Tiberius said, "but you know what bothers me? How the hell did Jetsu know that we had an X?"

"Well, history has proven that people on Quadrant Four can be bought for the right price."

"I don't buy that," Tiberius said. "They would've doubled down on security after last time."

"True," Spud said. "Any how did they know you were a Major or that Betty was our mom? They had intel on us."

"Maybe Jetsu is working for the navy," the Senator said.

Tiberius and Spud looked at him.

Their father shrugged. "You think governments around the world haven't armed terrorists in order to take out mutual threats. An enemy of my enemy, and all that. Guantano was a problem and he kept evading the navy, so they may have found someone who could sneak up on Guantano unawares."

"So, the navy told Jetsu to come and rob us?" Spud said.

"I don't buy that," Tiberius said. "Admiral Eames would not set us up. Lorenzo got shot for god's sake."

"Probably no one was meant to get hurt," the Senator said. "That's the problem with these operations. Once you arm an enemy, you can't control what they do with the power you grant them."

"Shit," Tiberius said, looking a little shocked. Or maybe disappointed.

"And you wonder why I left the military," Spud said to his brother.

"It's necessary," the Senator said. "Sometimes there's no other way."

"So, you get rid of one problem," Spud said, "but all you do is create another."

The Senator nodded. "Then we erase the second problem."

"At the expense of your soldiers."

"Not if we play it smart," his father said. "It's never our intention for casualties, Spelton."

"Yeah, well, the road to hell is paved with good intentions."

The two stared at each other in the dim light of the ceiling space.

"As much as I'd love to discuss politics with you both," Tiberius said, taking off the vent grate and tossing it aside, "I wouldn't mind getting out of this crawl space."

He ducked his head down and looked around to make sure it was clear, then moved to swing his legs through the hole and drop down to the floor. Spud passed him the sword then ushered his father forward. The Senator moved to dangle his legs through the hole, but then paused, looking back at Spud.

"I knew you'd make it off Bracken-Loti. That's why I agreed for you to be sent there. It was your only way out."

"I nearly died. So did Tim."

"But you didn't, because you were together. Because we Whitlams are stronger together."

"But I'm not a Whitlam, am I?" Spud said.

"Hurry up!" Tiberius hissed from below.

The Senator's face fell a little, then he turned and dropped through the hole.

● ● ●

The three men slunk along the corridor toward the elevators. They felt a series of vibrations through the ship, indicating pods leaving with evacuees. He hoped there'd be one left for them to get back to the *Benobi* with.

Spud checked his data-band. Still no comms.

The sound of banging rang out down the corridor from one of the elevators. The sound of someone trapped inside, trying to get out. They jogged to the doors and Spud hit the button to open them but with the power out they wouldn't open automatically.

"Nik," he said tapping on the doors, "is that you in there?"

"I am going to beat the *living* shit out of you!" her voice yelled from the other side.

Spud smiled with relief looking at his companions. "We found her!" He looked back to the doors. "We're going to get you out. Stand back."

"Hurry up!" she said. Spud noted her voice sounded like it was coming from below. He looked back at Tiberius. "I think they're stuck between floors. Help me."

The two men dug their fingers into the outer doors and pulled them apart. As Spud had suspected, the elevator was halfway between floors, which meant the team would only have a small gap to squeeze through to get out. Tiberius stabbed the sword between the inner doors and together they wrenched them apart. As they did, they saw Nikita, Finn, Glossy and Byron staring back at them, with two guards unconscious on the floor at their feet. Finn and Byron had the guards' weapons.

"Nice work," Spud said, motioning to the unconscious guards.

"Shut up and get us out of here!" Nikita said, raising her arms to them. Tiberius and Spud took an arm each and hauled her through the gap to their floor.

Nikita found her feet beside the Senator. "You must be—" she began, before the brothers cut her off.

"Our father," Tiberius said, while Spud answered, "The Senator."

The Senator noticed, throwing Spud a glance. Spud ignored it as he and Tiberius reached back through and pulled Glossy out, then Byron, then Finn. As Finn got to his feet, he clapped Spud on the shoulder.

"Good to see you, brother."

"Good to see you too," Spud smiled, clapping his shoulder too.

"Alright," Nikita said, "let's get back to the ship and get the hell out of here!"

"We gotta get Lulu!" Spud said.

"We'll get her on the way," Glossy said.

"Stairs," Spud said, pointing toward them and leading the way.

● ● ●

Spud led the pack, slinking silently down the stairs to the main casino floor. He paused, though, when just past the base of the stairs they saw the bloodied, mangled body of one of the casino patrons—their chest and neck shredded. He looked to Tiberius and the sword he carried.

"We need more weapons," he said, then looked back to Finn and Byron. "Finn, take the rear, Byron, get up here," then he turned to Tiberius again. "Go guard the Senator."

"You mean Dad," Tiberius said, shooting him a look, then dropping back to take the Senator's side.

Byron stepped up beside Spud. The weapon she had was only a guard's tazer, but it would do. Spud thought about the tranq gun the guard had mentioned but had no idea where it was located.

"Slow and steady," Spud said, stepping out with her by his side, and making their way toward the next set of stairs that led down to the cargo hold.

Just as he hit the top of the stairs, though, the *meow* sounded. Spud and Byron froze then slowly turned their faces in the direction it had come from. There, coming around the corner at the end of the corridor was the Panthera dragging a man's body.

A body whose eyes pleaded with theirs as they mouthed: "Help me."

Spud suddenly realized who it was.

"Guantano," he whispered.

"Spud?" Tiberius said, sliding up beside him. Spud watched as Guantano continued to play dead as he was dragged by the X, his eyes pleading for help.

Spud sighed. "Fuck. I can't let him go out this way." He looked at Tiberius. "He's my father."

"You don't owe him anything."

"Get the others to Lulu and start evacuating to the *Benobi*," Spud said, grabbing the sword Tiberius carried. "I'll take the next one."

"Spud?" Finn said, joining them. "We're not leaving without you."

"Get Lulu," he said, then started running toward the Panthera. "HEY!" he yelled, banging the sword on the walls.

The Panthera stopped dragging Guantano and turned its skin-covered eyes to him.

Its pink furless ears went back and it crouched ready to lunge, giving that terrifying growl.

But an explosion threw it off guard, shaking Spud and his companions off their feet. The lights dimmed, then blinked back on, as the Panthera switched to camouflage and began to bound toward them.

"Oh shit!" Spud yelled. "Run! Run!"

Nikita and Glossy headed down the stairs, and Tiberius pushed the Senator after them, but Byron and Finn held steady with their tazers, firing at the mirage headed toward them.

They missed at first, but then Byron caught it. A blue electrical field swam over it, before its camouflage dropped away and the Panthera skidded to the ground. Spud held his sword firm, but Tiberius pushed it down.

"We have to return it alive!"

"What?" Spud looked at his brother like he was crazy.

"I promised the admiral!"

"So!"

"So, it's our way out, Spud. We return it *alive*. Hurry!" Tiberius began to move swiftly toward it. "Byron!" he called to his soldier, who moved quickly to his side.

The Panthera was down, but not out, trembling as though trying to shake the immobilizing charge from itself.

While Byron, Finn and Tiberius stood before the Panthera, Spud slinked past them toward Guantano, still laying on the ground in the intersecting corridor, his legs shredded and bleeding. As Spud knelt down beside him, he caught movement around the corner of the intersecting corridor that scared the shit out of him.

"Godammit!" Spencer yelled in fright, weapon aimed at him about to shoot.

"Shit!" Spud quickly raised his hands, then lowered them again. "We don't have much time! Hurry!" Spud moved to lift Guantano's torso while Spencer grabbed his legs and then began to carry him back along the corridor toward the stairs.

"It's getting back to its feet!" Byron yelled.

"Hold!" Tiberius said, hands out. "Too much charge might kill it!"

"Yeah, well it's the Panthera or us!" Byron said.

The Panthera struggled, shaking its body, its camouflage turning on and off.

Then it growled and suddenly came to life.

"Shit!" Byron fired at it, but missed as it swiftly darted to the side. Finn fired and he missed too, as it sped past him and seemed to circle them before leaping onto Byron and knocking her down, then doing the same with Finn, blood spraying from claw wounds as the creature used their bodies to propel itself onward.

"Fuck!" Tiberius yelled, taking chase, but the Panthera was back to normal now, running up the walls and dodging the tazer fire expertly.

And it was *pissed*.

Like a rocket it came barreling back toward Spud, along the floor, up the wall, all the while in its mirage-like form, hard to pinpoint.

Spencer dropped Guantano's legs and quickly raised his weapon, but he was too slow. The Panthera leaped on him, grabbing him by the neck and knocking him down in a spray of blood.

"SHIT!" Spud said, grabbing onto Guantano tighter and dragging his body toward the stairs. "Run! Get out of here!" he yelled to the others.

Tiberius pulled Byron to her feet, the side of her body bleeding from deep claw wounds, while Nikita and Glossy crept back from the stairs to grab Finn.

The Panthera shook Spencer's body violently until it was sure he was dead, then it turned back to Spud, blood dripping from its mouth. It snarled and prepared to pounce again.

"Shit! Shit! Shit!" he yelled, heaving Guantano along.

"Leave him!" Tiberius yelled.

"No! I'm your father! Please!" Guantano pleaded.

"Get out of the *goddamn* way!" an angel's voice sounded.

Spud glanced back to see Grey step out from the stairs in full battle gear, aiming her weapon at the creature. Spud threw himself against the wall as she fired. The creature tried to dodge the fire but caught a bullet in its hind quarters. It yelped and spun and raced back to the corner in the corridor for shelter.

Spud, panting, looked back at Grey. "You found us. Again."

Grey glanced at him. "Someone had to come and save your ass."

Spud smiled like a drooling baby. "God, I love you."

Grey paused, as did everyone else, before she continued: "Get the hell up, and go down to the cargo hold," she said. "Transport's waiting to get us off."

"Yes, ma'am," he said, grabbing Guantano once more, as the Panthera peered around the corner at them, now looking extremely pissed. Its black eyes beneath that pink skin looked as evil as could be.

"What about the Panthera?" Tiberius said from the top of the stairs, still holding Byron. "We need it alive."

Grey looked at him.

"Admiral's orders," Tiberius said.

Grey looked back to the Panthera. "Shit."

"We need to lure it back to the box," Tiberius said.

"Get the wounded to the ship. We'll deal with that later," Grey said, backing up as the Panthera disappeared again.

They made their way down to the cargo hold level, dragging and carrying their wounded, while Grey provided cover.

"Did you bring back-up?" Spud asked her.

She kept her eyes fixed on the corridor.

"Where are they?" Spud asked.

"Back on my ship."

"You boarded alone?"

She nodded. "I'm not risking any of my crew again. I made that mistake last time."

Spud smiled sadly, as he continued to drag Guantano. "That's not how a soldier works, Grey," he said quietly.

"Yeah, well, this isn't official business," she said. "I'm supposed to be chasing Jetsu."

"But you came here instead?" Spud asked, surprised.

She threw him a glance as they reached the cargo hold. "Apparently so."

Spud's face softened as he stared at her. "I am buying you the biggest, best, goddamn dinner you've ever had when this is over."

Guantano laughed. "*Boy*, you've got it bad! Just like your mother. A fool for love. Or should I say, *lust*."

Grey turned her gun to Guantano. "This is your father?"

"Unfortunately," Spud said.

"We could just leave him here," Grey said flatly.

"Blood is thicker than water, sweetheart," Guantano smiled. "He came back to get me."

"Well, not really," Spud said. "The Panthera actually brought you to us. It didn't want you either."

"That's right," the Senator said, moving toward them. He stared down at Guantano. "He came back to save *me*."

"Enough of this bullshit!" Spud snapped. "Stop making me a pawn in your game of superiority like you did with mom."

"Spud!" Tiberius came running back, his shirt stained with Byron's blood. "The shuttle only takes four."

Spud thought for a moment and nodded. "Tell Nik to take the wounded, Byron and Finn, and take Glossy, and get the med bay and ship ready for departure."

"Glossy can wait," Tiberius said, "we send Dad instead."

"Hey, I'm wounded!" Guantano said, wincing as he reached for his cut legs.

"There's only room for one," the Senator said to Guantano.

The Panthera growled close by. Grey straightened and held her weapon firm, scanning the corridor beyond them.

Spud turned back to Tiberius. "Tell Nik to take Glossy and remote pilot the shuttle back to us."

"Spud?" Tiberius said.

"She's taking Glossy!" he repeated.

"Hurry up!" Grey barked. "The longer you talk about it the longer the Panthera has to eat us!"

Tiberius nodded, then turned to pass on the message.

Spud, out of the corner of his eye, saw the Senator staring at him. Spud turned to him.

"You said the Whitlams were stronger together," Spud said. "Now's your chance to prove it."

CHAPTER TWELVE

Spud made his father help carry Guantano into the cargo bay, to wait by the doors for the shuttle to return. Guantano was looking pale and sweating, his blood loss beginning to show, and no doubt the venom taking effect. Spud, further, made the Senator press rags against Guantano's wounds. Guantano was enjoying it. The Senator was not. But it told Spud something important. The Senator was doing as his stepson asked. He doubted if the situation had been reversed that Guantano would do the same.

Still, right now, Spud didn't have time to dwell on his two fathers. Right now, his priority was freeing Lulu from her box. As he pulled the lid off and placed it beside the box, he heard a growl.

"Oh, shit," he said. "You grew again?"

Lulu growled again and shook off the shed fur and skin, her ears pinned back.

"I know, I know," Spud said to her. "I'm a bad daddy and I promise I will *never* put you in a box again." He reached his hand in tentatively. She sniffed it, ears still pinned back. "Uh oh, you can smell the Panthera, can't you? I swear I'm not cheating on you, honey. That bitch tried to kill me, can you believe that?"

"He's gone insane," the Senator said watching him.

Lulu leaped out of the box into Spud's arms, who only managed to hold her briefly before dropping her—she was just too big and heavy now. Though she hadn't grown any more in height – she was still as tall as an Irish Wolfhound - but she *had* filled out a little, her lean limbs now more solid. Though in truth she was slightly smaller and less muscular than her lethal sister roaming the ship.

"He has an affinity with dangerous animals, just like his father," Guantano smiled in awe.

The Senator looked at Guantano and pressed his hands down harder on his wounds. Guantano gasped in pain.

"Truth hurt, Whitlam?" Guantano said.

"You're not his father."

"Wanna bet? Mrs. Whitlam can testify to that."

The Senator pushed harder on the wounds, making Guantano groan now.

"You're *not* his father," the Senator hissed. "You were never there for him. You never raised him. *I* did! *I* stood up and became the man you failed to be!"

"Yeah, but did you do it to save face?" Guantano asked. "Or did you do it to annoy me?"

"I did it because it was the right thing to do! I realized just how petty our fight had become for you to drag Betty into it. You're right, you know, I drove her to the affair, and I drove you to get back at me and he was the result," he said pointing at Spud, who knelt on the ground scratching Lulu's neck watching them. "Enough was enough! I knew it was time to grow up and be the man I should've been," the Senator seethed. "That's the difference between you and me, you know. You refused to grow up."

"Blow me!" Guantano said.

Grey suddenly strode from the door and stormed up to them both, aiming her weapon in their faces. "Blow your face off?" she asked as Tiberius quickly slipped to the door to take over her position. "Both of you shut up now, or I will personally feed you to the Panthera!" she said.

"She's feisty," Guantano said to Spud, who stood.

Grey moved her weapon closer to Guantano's face.

"I have the same taste in women as my son," he smiled at Grey.

"Eww," Spud said, screwing his face up.

He looked back at Spud. "You're a chip off the old block. You'll never be a Whitlam."

"He already is," Tiberius said firmly.

Spud looked at his brother, as Grey backed away again.

"I like how you're all so good at speaking for him," Grey said, locking eyes with Spud as she passed. She reached the door again and hiked her thumb at Tiberius to move. He did as ordered, despite being superior in rank. No one wanted to piss off Grey right now.

Lulu growled. Spud wasn't sure if it was through hunger or whether she sensed the Panthera close by.

"How long until the shuttle returns?" Tiberius asked Grey, as Spud petted Lulu again.

"I'd say a good twenty minutes," she said, glancing at her data-band and tapping it as though to get it working. "Can't tell until the comms are back up."

"Nik will sort it once she's at the *Benobi's* desk." Spud said, looking around. "Is there any food in here?"

"Kitchen's down the corridor," Guantano said.

Spud looked at Grey. "Lulu needs food."

Grey looked at Lulu and she meowed at Grey as though backing up what Spud said.

"We have to stay together," she said.

"We have to lure the Panthera into that box," Tiberius said.

"There's no way it's getting back in that box, Tim," Spud said.

"It will if we tranq it, or tazer it."

"Do you know how much that thing will weigh?"

"I don't care, Spud," Tiberius said. "We're not killing it. We are returning it alive, just like I promised."

"We can't lure it close until we get these two off," Spud said, motioning to his fathers.

Tiberius nodded. "Shuttle only fits four anyway. There's five of us."

"And Lulu," Spud said, glancing around again making the calculations. He shrugged. "We can fit. Lulu sits on your lap," he said to Tiberius, "and Grey sits on mi—" He stopped his sentence at the hard look Grey gave him. "Or... we can find another way," he said to her. "Hey, I'm happy to sit on your lap. It's just that I'm heavier than you, so I thought—"

"Shut up," she said.

"Yes, ma'am."

"Stop calling me ma'am."

"Alright."

Guantano laughed again, albeit pained. "Sounds like they're married already."

"What would you know about marriage?" the Senator said.

"We need to work out a plan," Tiberius cut off Guantano's response.

"What if we turn the box on its side," Spud said studying it. "We get it in there, then shut the lid and tip it back up."

"Small problem, the lid's busted," the Senator said, inspecting the X's box.

"Shit," Spud said, looking about. "What about Lulu's box? It could work."

"We'd have to be fast and need strength for that," Tiberius said. "There's not enough of us."

Spud looked to Grey. "Do you happen to have a tranq gun on your ship?"

Grey glanced at him, then away again. "We can't use that."

"Why not?"

"Because."

"Because, why?"

She glanced at him again. "Because it's on the ship, chasing Jetsu."

Spud stared at her, mouth gaping. "Wait. There's no navy out there?" he said pointing at the ship's hull. Grey shook her head, darting her eyes back to the corridor again.

"Shit," Tiberius muttered.

Spud stepped closer to Grey and lowered his voice. "You left your ship to come here?"

She glanced at him, then nodded.

"Holy shit," Spud said softly.

"So, I'm probably going to get court-martialed when this is over," she said.

Spud was still hung up on her earlier comment. "You jumped ship to come here and help us," he said softly.

"Yeah, I guess I'm an idiot."

"No, you're not. I've... *never* had a woman do something like that for me before. I mean, shit, my last girlfriend left me to be eaten by a Panthera and here you are coming to save me from one."

"I haven't saved you yet."

Spud smiled. "Yes, you have."

Grey looked at him and the two shared a moment, before she looked back at the audience, then turned back to the corridor again. Spud turned around to see Tiberius and his two fathers grinning at him. Spud flipped them the bird, then Lulu meowed again loudly. She was pissed and hungry.

"Shit, Spud," Tiberius said. "Lulu's going to bring the thing right here."

"Isn't that what we want?"

"Maybe. But only after the shuttle returns."

"Well, if I don't give Lulu food now, she's going to eat us all," Spud said, and Lulu meowed in return as though in agreement. "Give me the sword, I'm going to the kitchen."

"Take Lulu with you at least," Tiberius said.

"I'll come," Grey said.

"No," Spud shook his head. "You protect this lot."

"Hey," Tiberius said offended. "In that case, I'll come with you and Lulu."

Spud shrugged and moved to the door. "Which way?" he asked Guantano. His biological father pointed right down the corridor. Spud glanced back at Grey. "Back soon. Come on, Lulu."

● ● ●

Lulu trotted beside him, and Spud kept glancing at her to see if she detected the Panthera. Every now and then Lulu stopped and sniffed the air. Or her ears would twitch in all directions. Spud sensed the Panthera was close, but he wouldn't panic until Lulu hissed her warning.

Spud's data-band suddenly lit up, signaling Nik was at the *Benobi's* flight desk and had opened the comms channel to him.

15 minutes ETA for shuttle. Nik messaged him.

Roger. He tapped back into his data-band then quickly relayed the message to Grey, along with: *We made the kitchen.*

Grey typed back: *Hurry.*

Spud: Roger that.

Lulu meowed loudly again.

Tiberius looked at her and raised his finger to his lips. "Shhh!"

Spud moved past his brother to the fridges and opened them. "Watch the door," he said, placing his sword on the bench.

Tiberius positioned himself in the doorway, as Spud rummaged quickly and quietly through the fridge for food. He pulled out a big bowl of mince and grinned.

"Don't say daddy doesn't love you, honey," he said to Lulu, putting the bowl on the floor. Lulu immediately tucked in.

Spud looked back in the fridge. "Alright!" he whispered, pulling out a small clear plastic container holding a mini-cheesecake. "Want one?"

Tiberius gave him an incredulous look, but then shrugged and nodded. "Okay."

Spud tossed him one and Tiberius quickly shoved it in his mouth. Spud pulled another out, then decided to shove it in his pocket. "Better take one for Grey."

Just as he reached in for another for himself, Lulu hissed viciously. Spud dropped the container and spun around. Lulu was hissing up at the ceiling. He glanced over at Tiberius who was now aiming his tazer up at the roof.

"It's between us," his brother whispered, gauging where Lulu's eyes were focused.

Lulu hissed again and the Panthera growled back.

"I don't suppose you want to share that bowl, Lulu?" Spud whispered to her.

Lulu hissed in response.

"Spud!" Tiberius whispered. "Get over here now!"

Spud nodded and pressed himself up against the bench as he reached out for the sword. As he neared the air vent, however, he paused. He just made out the ghostly shape of the Panthera's pale pink face and the black holes where the eyes stared back at him.

"Fuck," Spud muttered under his breath. It was a terrifying image.

He snatched up the sword and moved back to Lulu who continued to stare at the vent, ears pinned back and teeth bared.

"Lulu, I need that meat." He reached down carefully, slowly, and picked up the bowl, then began moving back toward the vent.

Lulu growled and the Panthera growled back, swiping its paws at the grate and knocking it off to the floor.

"I think we're about to have the literal definition of a cat fight," Tiberius said quietly.

"No, we're not," Spud said, moving slowly with the bowl. "It's not touching Lulu. She's a lover not a fighter. Just like her dad." Spud carefully placed the bowl on the bench near the vent, then stepped backward. "Lulu, go to Uncle Tim," he pointed at the door.

Lulu dug in, tensing her muscles and growling at the vent.

"Lulu!" he hissed quietly. "Uncle Tim. *Now!*"

"Lulu!" Tiberius called, tapping his thigh.

"Lulu!" Spud pointed to this brother.

"Spud, just get here and she'll follow!"

"Damn it!" Spud began to cross the room but saw the Panthera moving its body around watching him. "Just eat the damn meat, would you!" he said, pointing to the bowl.

The Panthera snarled viciously. Lulu snarled in reply.

"Tim," Spud said. "On the count of three we run."

"And go where? The shuttle's not here yet."

"We just gotta hold it back until we can board."

"What about putting it back in the box?"

"Tim? Fuck the box. And fuck the Panthera. If the navy want it then they can come tranq it themselves."

"I was ordered—"

"Not to kill it. We haven't, it's still alive. Technically the navy can come get it, which means it's returned," he said as the cats continued to growl and hiss at each other in the background.

"Grey wounded it."

"To save a life."

"Spud, I said it would never leave the box."

"Tim, I am running on three," Spud said impatiently. "You can run as well, or I will run over you. Understood?"

"I'm going to beat your ass when we get out of here," his brother replied, eyes still fixed on the vent.

"Join the queue."

Tiberius scoffed. "You'll be hiding behind Grey anyway."

"Yes, I will. *Happily*. Now RUN!"

Spud raced for the door, hitting it just as Tiberius left it.

"Lulu!" Spud barked as he raced down the corridor. He heard a loud bang and more growling and turned round to see Lulu shoot out of the kitchen after them, with the Panthera not far behind.

Spud turned back to see Tiberius stop, turn around and aim his tazer.

"Move!" Tiberius yelled, and Spud threw himself to the side as his brother fired. He hit the creature and once more it skidded to the ground, trying to shake off its tazed body lock.

"What the hell's going on?" Grey called, peering out of the cargo bay doorway ahead.

"Incoming!" Spud called running past Tiberius toward her. He came to a stop before her, panting, as Lulu raced into the cargo hold, and Tiberius joined him at the door.

"How long until it's back up and running?" Grey asked, studying the Panthera shaking off the effects of the tazer.

"I'd say we've got about two minutes, max," Spud said. "Get ready to load the shuttle."

"I could kill it," she said, holding her weapon firm.

"No!" Tiberius said. "I'll taze it again if we have to."

"My brother, military man through and through, obeying orders."

"Hey!" Tiberius said, "I'm trying to keep you out of jail."

They heard a loud clunk as a shuttle locked with *Bandora's Star*. Spud nervously checked his data-band. "Nikita, I love you!" he said.

The Panthera was back on its feet shaking off the last of the effects of the tazer.

"Shit!" Tiberius said raising his weapon again.

The hatch to the shuttle opened—operated by Nik from the *Benobi*.

"Get them aboard!" Tiberius yelled.

Spud raced inside to lift Guantano. "Help me!" the called to the Senator, who did so. "Hold this," he said, throwing his sword to Guantano.

They lifted Guantano into the shuttle and placed him in one of the seats, then moved back to the shuttle's door.

"Eve! Tim! Get back here!" Spud yelled, the Senator by his side.

"Coming!" Tiberius said, firing his tazer at the creature again, then suddenly his eyes dropped to the ground. "Oh, shit."

"What?" Spud ran toward them. He saw the Panthera was on the ground, unmoving. "Shit! Is it dead?"

"I think we tazed it too much," Tiberius said.

"Hey!" they heard the Senator yell and looked back to the shuttle. The Senator was on the ground holding the back of his head and Guantano stood there holding the sword.

"What the...?" Spud said.

"You never asked if I could walk," Guantano shrugged and smiled. "I hurt my legs falling down the stairs in the panic, landed in shards of glass. I played dead when the cat started dragging me, then you showed up. Fate, son." He stepped back inside the shuttle. "I'm sorry I can't take you with me."

"Oh, no." Spud's face fell. "No! No! No!" He ran for the shuttle but Guantano closed the hatch door. Spud banged on the hatch. "You son of a bitch!"

"Oh shit!" Tiberius yelled.

Spud looked back to see the Panthera leap for Tiberius and Grey, knocking them down. Lulu hissed and raced toward them.

"Fuck!" Spud yelled, torn between the corridor and the shuttle. He ran toward the corridor, and saw Lulu clamp her jaw on the Panthera's already wounded rear. "No, Lulu!" he yelled, pulling Grey to her feet as Tiberius got to his. They both had bleeding claw marks, but they would both live. Spud grabbed Tiberius' tazer off the floor and aimed it at the Panthera. "Lulu! Let go!"

He heard the sound of the shuttle unclamping from *Bandora's Star.*

"Lulu!" he yelled again as the Panthera twisted and turned, swiping at Lulu. Its claws finally caught her, Lulu whined and let go. Spud took aim and fired.

The tazer hit its target and locked up the creature's muscles again. Tiberius swooped in and picked up Lulu, then raced back into the cargo hold.

"Let me kill it!" Grey said, taking aim.

"No!" Tiberius yelled.

"Get back!" Spud said, pushing her inside the cargo hold.

"Try the box!" the Senator's voice sounded. "It's our only shot!"

Spud looked back to see his father pull Lulu's box out from the wall and try to tip it.

"Help me!" his father yelled, and Tiberius and Grey positioned themselves either side and tipped the box over.

Spud watched as the Panthera got to its feet again, shaking its body, its legs, its head.

"It's on its feet!" Spud yelled.

"We need bait!" his father said.

The Panthera snarled at Spud and he swiftly turned and swooped back into the room. As he did, they heard another clunk and saw the shuttle was locking on again. He saw Guantano's shocked face.

Spud smiled. "Yeah, that's right. Nikita's remotely controlling the shuttle, *asshole!*"

"Spud!" Grey yelled and he turned back to see the Panthera in the doorway, snarling.

Behind them the shuttle's door opened.

"Fuck!" they heard Guantano say as the Panthera lunged.

Spud dove aside, pushing Lulu out of the way, as Grey, Tiberius and the Senator, threw themselves behind Lulu's box and the Panthera went for easiest target available – hitting Guantano front on.

He screamed as the Panthera growled and clawed, and blood splashed up over the observation window. Spud flinched in shock.

"Spud!" Tiberius whispered urgently. Spud looked away from the carnage to see his brother and father heaving the box around to face the Panthera. Spud and Grey quickly joined them, pushing the box up against the shuttle's door.

Spud tapped the comms link on his data-band. "Nik, shut the hatch door halfway. Lock it there!"

"On it!" she replied.

They watched the hatch door descend and lock in place.

"Pull the box back a little," the Senator said. "Leave a gap for the lid."

They did so, while Spud scuttled over to collect the lid.

Soon enough, the Panthera became bored with Guantano's lifeless body and looked for an escape.

Lulu leaped painfully up on top of the box and growled through the window at the Panthera. It growled back and moved toward the box, sniffing it. Sensing it was trapped, it growled again. Spud passed the lid to his father, then got behind the box and knocked on it.

"Come on!" he said to the Panthera. "Come try and get to me!"

The Panthera growled again. Spud looked up at Lulu.

"Lulu, get down," he said, patting the ground. "Make it chase you."

Lulu painfully jumped down beside him.

The Panthera growled again, then there was a bang as Spud felt the box move—the Panthera trying to ram its way through to them.

"Get ready with the lid!" Tiberius yelled to his father.

The box shoved into Spud and Lulu again as the Panthera continued to ram. Spud quickly got to his feet to help Grey and Tiberius push back on the box and keep it in place. As soon as the Panthera was fully inside the box, the Senator slid the lid down.

"Lid on!" the Senator yelled. "How do I lock it?"

The Panthera rattled the box violently, desperately seeking a way out.

"Er…" Spud strained as he pushed back on the box, not sure how Glossy had worked the digital lock before.

"Dammit! Push it against the wall!" the Senator said, and together they heaved the violent shaking mass along the floor, away from the shuttle hatch, so that it sat, lid closed and flush against the hull of the ship.

They all took a moment to catch their breath, panting, before the box shook violently again.

"Shit," Spud said, "push some cargo against it."

While Spud and Grey pressed the box against the wall, Tiberius and their father moved to heave more boxes over against it to keep it wedged against the wall. Soon enough, a solid mound of cargo was stacked against the box, trapping it tightly against the wall, while the Panthera growled angrily.

Finally, when they were sure the Panthera wasn't going to escape, they all collapsed in exhausted, sweating and partially bloodied heaps.

Eventually, Spud looked at Grey. "Are you okay?" he said, reaching out to her bloodied arm. She nodded, panting. He smiled at her, then got to his feet and moved to look inside the shuttle.

There lay Guantano, throat and torso torn open. Dead.

Spud felt a presence come to stand beside him. It was the Senator.

"I'm sorry," he said.

"Are you?" Spud asked. He looked back at Guantano. "I'm not," he said. "The son of a bitch was going to leave me again."

The Senator gave a sympathetic smile and wrapped his arm around Spud's back, squeezing his shoulder.

Spud looked back at the Senator. "But you never did."

The Senator turned Spud toward him and pulled him into a hug. "I'm sorry I was so hard on you... I just didn't want you to turn out like him."

Spud pulled back from the hug. "And I didn't. Because of you."

"Told you you were a Whitlam," Tiberius smiled, clapping them both on the shoulder. They all grinned.

Lulu meowed again then and Spud looked back to see her licking her wounds as Grey crouched down beside her to examine them.

"Let's get the hell off this ship, huh?" Spud said, moving over to pick up Lulu, while Tiberius removed Guantano's body into the cargo hold.

They began piling into the shuttle. The Senator and Tiberius took the back two seats and Spud placed Lulu in a third, putting the belt on carefully across her wounds, before realizing there was just one seat left. He looked at Grey, then stepped aside and ushered her forward.

"I'll wait for the next one," he said.

"You'll wait?" she said.

He nodded at her and smiled. "As long as it takes."

She grabbed his shirt in her fist and pulled him forward, then pushed him down into the seat.

"Buckle up," she said, turning back for the door.

Spud knew better than to argue with her, so he buckled up, but when he looked back, she was shutting the shuttle door from the inside. She looked at him.

"And make some room," she motioned to his lap.

Spud smiled. "Yes, ma'— I mean, Lieutenant Grey."

She shot him a firm look as she turned her back to him and sat down on his lap. Spud fought a smile.

"I'm... going to need to put my arms around you," he said. "We have to buckle up. I don't make the rules, I just follow 'em."

Tiberius chuckled in the back, shaking his head.

Grey shot Spud another firm look, then took his wrists and wrapped his arms around her waist. He let his smile run free as she rested back against his chest.

Spud gave the thumbs-up sign to the camera in the shuttle. And Nikita began to bring them back to the *Benobi*.

CHAPTER THIRTEEN

Spud stood on the *Benobi*'s flight deck and stared out at the *Gabriel* floating before them.

"The admiral has asked for us to attend the ship," Glossy said.

Spud nodded as the Senator appeared beside him.

"Let me handle this," the Senator said.

Spud looked at him.

"This is what I do, Spelton," he said. "Let me handle the admiral."

"Well, now that depends," Spud said, "because if you bargain me and Tim into going to another planet like Bracken-Loti, I'm sorry, but I will speak for myself."

"I'm sorry," the Senator said in earnest. "I didn't know I was sending you down there to that. I was told they were feral cats. I wasn't told the severity of the creature."

Spud studied him, seeking the truth.

"Whatever you think of me," the Senator said, "do you really think I'd send my sons to their deaths to avoid a scandal?"

"You didn't send Tim, he volunteered. And I wasn't your son."

The Senator stared at him. "Yes, you were, Spelton. And I meant what I said before. I'm sorry if I never made you feel like you were. I pushed you hard because I didn't want you to end up like your father. If you were going to bear the Whitlam name, I wanted you to be like a Whitlam... I've made mistakes and I can't turn back the clock. But if you let me, we can move forward. Together."

Spud sighed, staring out at the *Gabriel*. "I can't let you speak for me," he finally said. "We'll go in together, but I speak for myself."

The Senator stared at him a moment then relented with a nod. "Okay." Then he smiled. "I *am* proud of you, Spelton. I am."

Spud nodded back. "And I did it my way. Not yours. I'm not Tiberius. I'll never be Tiberius. I'm just Spud. And I'm happy with that."

Glossy cleared her throat then. Spud looked at her and saw her eyes shining.

"We'd better get moving, huh?" she said gently.

"Yeah," Spud exhaled. "Call everyone together."

Spud sat at the *Gabriel*'s boardroom table with his

Benobi crew, Grey, Tiberius and his father. Byron was in the med bay, currently in a coma as the anti-venom did its thing, while Lorenzo was still recovering from his bullet wound on Nirvana Springs.

Admiral Eames and his aides sat facing them.

"I have a lot to process," the admiral said. "And there are a lot of decisions to be made..." His eyes were fixed on Grey for the last part.

"We understand that," the Senator said smoothly. "And please note I am happy to go on the record as to how admirably Major Whitlam, Mr. Compton, Lieutenant Grey, Sergeant Byron, and the members of the *Benobi* crew, acted. I wouldn't be sitting here, admiral, if they hadn't taken the brave actions they had."

"That will be noted, yes."

"And it's important to record that although the Panthera was mildly wounded, it is still alive, and the wounding was only done as a necessary course of action to save lives at the time."

"And it's in a box, still on *Bandora's Star*?"

"Yes," the Senator nodded.

"May I speak, sir?" Spud said, and the admiral gave him a nod. "Our recommendation for taking the Panthera back into custody is to first gas the cargo hold. That way, when they right the box the X will be at least groggy if not knocked out. The box is unlocked, and that's why it's on its side and wedged against the wall with cargo."

The admiral stared at him a moment, then nodded. "Noted."

"It should also please the navy that the gangster, Guantano, is dead, admiral," the Senator said. "And his secret gambling ship, *Bandora's Star*, can be shut down and all illegal activities ceased."

"Yes, but Jetsu managed to get away," the admiral said, turning his eyes once more to Grey.

"That may be so, sir," the Senator said, "but if Lieutenant Grey hadn't arrived when she did, either we would be dead or the Panthera would be. I guess it's a matter of what is more important to the navy, sir? The live Panthera, or Jetsu on the loose but who, in time, you can apprehend."

"Noted, Senator."

"I will be heavily pushing for a full pardon for all parties," the Senator said firmly.

"To be expected," the admiral said, his face giving nothing away.

"I will also be recommending an inquiry as to how Jetsu found out that the *Benobi* was carrying the Panthera-X03 in the first place, sir," the Senator said. "This was a top-secret mission, was it not? I am assured the leak did not come from those on the *Benobi*, which means the leak came from the navy side, sir. Whether that was on Quadrant Four, or here on the *Gabriel*, is to be determined."

Spud glanced at his father in contained awe but kept his emotion internal. He'd been adamant he wasn't going to let his father speak for him, but now... Spud felt he'd just let his father go for it.

Though Spud contained his emotion, the admiral allowed himself a small smile. "There's the Senator I know. You were always one for playing hardball, weren't you?"

The Senator smiled and shrugged. "I just think civilians of the world might like to know why the life of the hero soldier, Timothy Tiberius Whitlam, was put at risk by the navy leak. Not to mention my own life, a long supporter of the military. If that were to get out, there would be an outcry. I think it's best for all that we deal with this in-house, don't you?"

"I will take that under consideration," the admiral said. "Is that all?"

The Senator nodded. "For now, yes."

"Very well," the admiral said. "You are all dismissed. However, for the time being, you will all remain on or close to the *Gabriel*. Am I clear?"

"Absolutely!" the Senator smiled.

"Good," the admiral said, "You're dismissed." He quickly turned his eyes to Grey. "If you could stay, lieutenant?"

She nodded as everyone stood. Spud threw her a concerned look, but her face gave nothing away.

● ● ●

Spud sat on the floor by Lulu's bed, petting her after redressing her wounds. Though she wasn't quite herself, she did seem to appreciate the pats and scratches he gave her. He'd been worried at first, wondering what affect the X's venom might have on her, but of course, as she was half X, he needn't have worried.

A knock sounded on the door. He stood and answered it. It was Grey.

"Hey," he said, opening the door wider to let her in, "what happened?"

She exhaled heavily as she stepped inside and he closed the door behind her. "I'm being stood down pending a hearing."

"Shit," he said, "I'm sorry."

She shrugged. "I'm not."

"You're not?"

She shook her head. "I don't really know what I want anymore." She moved over and crouched down to pet Lulu, her mind wandering. "I've been lost for a while, stuck patrolling The Wastelands, wondering what I'm doing with my life... I don't know. Some time out might be good."

He smiled. "Well, I'm down some crew if you want to join the *Benobi*?"

She looked at him.

"The admiral offered to make the *Benobi* an official cargo carrier for Quadrant Four," he shrugged. "I guess we've seen it now and have the knowledge. The navy might as well use us."

She smiled back, standing again. "Maybe."

"Although we don't often get the chance to shoot people. You might get bored."

She chuckled and nodded. "Maybe."

"So, I guess if you're on indefinite leave," Spud said stepping toward her, "you've got all the time in the world for that dinner, huh?" He held up his hand. "Wait!" He ran over to a small cooler in the corner of his cabin and pulled out the little cheesecake he took off *Bandora's Star* and presented it to her. "Dessert!"

A smile spread across her face as she looked at it.

"Sorry," he said, studying the dented plastic container. "It got a little battered in transit."

Her smile faded to a serious look. "About that. Dessert."

Spud paused. "Oh, shit." He lowered his offering. "You just said that so I'd stay alive on Bracken-Loti."

She gave him a look like he was an idiot. "You think I'd just say something like that?"

He shrugged. "I don't know."

She stepped closer to him. "I was actually thinking that we should get to that dinner sooner rather than later, before something else crops up to keep us from it."

A grin swept across his face. "Oh! Good." He stepped closer to her.

"In fact," she said, stepping even closer to him, "I think maybe we should just cut straight to dessert. I mean, anything could happen, right?"

He nodded, taking a moment to get his mouth to work. "Ab-absolutely."

He stepped forward again and the two stood right in front of each other.

"So..." she said.

"So..." he said back, glancing down at the cheesecake. "You want—"

"No."

Spud threw the cheesecake over his shoulder. "Okay."

She smiled. "Shut up and kiss me, Spud."

"Yes, ma'am," he leaned forward and they kissed. It was soft and warm and gentle, but it soon became more than that as she pressed her body against his, wrapped her arms around his neck, and he wrapped his arms around her back, squeezing her tighter against him.

Then his data-band signaled an incoming call.

He quickly killed the call. "No."

They continued kissing.

Then her data-band signaled a call. She looked at it worried.

"No..." she said killing it.

They looked at each other, concerned.

"We don't have much time," she said.

"I'm okay with that if you are."

She nodded and pulled off her shirt. "Let's go!"

"Yes, ma'am!" he said, pulling his shirt off too. They reconnected and moved backward toward his bed. Just as they lay down she grabbed his arms.

"Spud! Door. Lock it!"

"Yes! Shit." He sprang up, raced for the door, locked it and raced back to pull off her boots and trousers, then his own, then get on the bed again.

Then the comms panel above his bed, signaled an alert.

"Goddamn!" he said, smacking his hand against it to kill it.

"Hurry!" she said, underwear flying.

They reconnected, just as Lulu meowed, not once but twice. Spud looked at her, staring at them.

"Lulu, turn around, face the wall!" he pointed.

Grey pulled his face back to hers as her data-band sounded again.

"No, no, no, no!" she said taking it off and throwing it across the room. She looked back at Spud. "We are having dessert, goddamn it!"

He nodded. "I have *never* wanted dessert more in my entire life."

Spud kissed her again, as they blocked out the world around them and drowned themselves within.

Thanks for reading! If you enjoyed reading *The Deftest Deceit* (Spud Compton 3), let people know! Leave a simple rating or write a brief review wherever you can. It means a lot to the author and really helps with making this book visible to others.

And if you're looking for another military sci-fi series – one that is a little darker – then check out **Aurora: Darwin**, the first book in the Aurora series:

Aurora: Darwin (Aurora 1)

When a distress signal is received from a black-ops space station on the edge of inhabited space, Captain Saul Harris of the UNF *Aurora* is called in from leave to respond. But the mission is not what it seems. Information is thin on the ground and three new recruits have been added to the Aurora crew. For Corporal Carrie Welles, one of the Aurora's new recruits, her first mission in space seems like a dream come true. Determined to achieve the success of her father before her, and suddenly thrust into a terrifying mission, she must work with her new captain and the strained *Aurora* crew to make it home alive. When the Aurora arrives at the station, Harris and Welles soon find themselves caught up in a desperate fight for survival. Station Darwin is not what they expected. The lights are off, but somebody is home...

If you like the sound of a near future crime thriller, check out **The Subjugate** – now being developed for TV!

The Subjugate (Salvation 1)

In a small religious community rocked by a spree of shocking murders, Detectives Salvi Brentt and Mitch Grenville find themselves surrounded by suspects. The Children of Christ have a tight grip on their people, and the Solme Complex neurally edit violent criminals - Subjugates - into placid servants called Serenes. In a town where purity and sin, temptation and repression live side by side, everyone has a motive. But as the bodies mount up, the frustrated detectives begin to crack under the pressure: their demons come to light, and who knows where the blurred line between man and monster truly lies...

MORE BY AMANDA BRIDGEMAN

Marvel: Sound of Light [Marvel X-Men Universe]

When rock star Dazzler walked out on S.H.I.E.L.D., she hoped she'd seen the last of the clandestine organization. But when a rogue agent drops in after a sold-out gig, she must decide whether to work with them again or stick to her solo career. The agent links Mutant Growth Hormone – a dangerous biochemical that wildly enhances mutant powers – with the disappearance of Magneto and Cyclops. Reluctantly, Dazzler takes the case and unfolds a mystery greater than she anticipated. In need of a new team, she recruits the extraordinary mutants Emma Frost, Polaris, and Rachel Grey on a mission to foil a plot to remove mutantkind forever, which blasts them from Earth into a whole new dimension.

Pandemic: Patient Zero [Medical Procedural Thriller]
Bodhi Patel is the brand new Lead Epidemiologist for the world's top epidemic specialists, Global Health Agency, but there's no time to settle in: his new boss, Helen Taylor, deploys GHA to contain a mysterious new killer virus spreading from Peru into Brazil. On the ground they learn that the virus is loose in a region controlled by a heavily armed drug warlord, and the race against time to discover a cure just got a whole lot tougher. Meanwhile, Bodhi finds himself with a newly reshuffled team still smarting from the changes, including his ex – the last person he expected to be working with. Based on the smash hit boardgame, *Pandemic*, and winner of the *Scribe Award* for Best Novel - General!

The Time of the Stripes [Grounded Sci-Fi Thriller]
No-one had heard of Victoryville before. But when an alien spaceship appears, hovering over the town, the whole world suddenly knows its name. After twenty-four hours and a failed military assault, the ship disappears without a trace. When the outside world restores communication to the town, thousands are reported missing. Those who remain in Victoryville are irreparably changed. However, only some have been left with strange red marks upon their skin. Quarantined from the outside world and segregated within, alliances are made and relationships are shattered, as everyone fights for the truth - and for their own survival. *The Time of the Stripes* is a powerful sci-fi thriller!